Ever Since that Day

EMMA ABRAHAMS

Ever Since that Day
ISBN 978-0-473-70011-9

Published by Midnight Pixel Studios Ltd

Text copyright © 2023 Emma Abrahams.
Illustration copyright © 2023 Create Design Studio,
Aotearoa | New Zealand
Revised edition
Cover illustration: Caitlin Tindall, Create Design Studio

This is a work of fiction. All of the characters, organisations, and events
portrayed in this novel are either products of the author's imagination or are
used fictitiously. Any resemblance to actual persons, living or dead, events or
locales is entirely coincidental.

For Paul.
I love you inside and out.

One

"Oh, no you don't." Skye Fletcher knocked my hand away from the ponytail I'd been securing with a black hair-tie.

"Oi!" I exclaimed as the hair-tie pinged out of my grasp. With hair tumbling down to my waist, I spun around from the dressing table to glare at my best friend. "What was that for?"

"Whoops. Sorry, Nova," Skye apologised, sounding genuine, although the glint in her brown eyes gave her away. "But seriously. It's your birthday and I'm banning you from ponytails. You and ponytails are breaking up. Please, for the love of all things holy, do something spectacular with those luscious locks of yours."

"Why? It's just going to be you and the boys here. Same as ever." I gave the obvious excuse for why I kept my hair so plain – the excuse Skye needed to hear. It was a slippery slope, and I knew that if I gave in to my desires, I'd quickly spiral into someone I didn't want to be.

Skye, however, was not to be deterred. She flung open my wardrobe doors and announced, "This is the only time we get to celebrate you turning 17. Surely that's a good enough reason for you to wear this." She pulled out a frothy blue dress from between the row of school uniforms, holding it up to my bedroom light like it was the anointed one.

The thought of wearing such a beautiful dress tonight – of trying not to look for a reaction from *him* when he saw me in that floating concoction, which brought out the blue in my eyes and transformed my lanky figure into something soft and alluring – went against everything I had been working towards for the past year. So, I did what I always did these days – I deflected.

Pointing my brush at Skye, I narrowed my eyes and said, "This is a ploy, isn't it? You're trying to hook me up with Matthias! Just because the guy's taller than me, doesn't mean I have to go out with him."

"Oh, heck no!" Skye held up her small hands. "I know you're not into Matthias! I'd never do that to you."

Still on edge, I resorted to the jokester persona I'd been cultivating lately and asked, "So… why *are* you gunning to give me a *Princess Diaries* makeover?"

Skye snorted and said, "You are not in need of a makeover. You're gorgeous exactly as you are – active wear and all. However, it just so happens that on this one, highly-momentous, never-to-be repeated occasion, I think you should dress up. Okay?"

"Fine." I rolled my eyes, even as I felt my heartbeat speed up. "Do what you want with me."

"Excellent!" Skye grinned, drumming the tips of her fingers together joyfully while her golden curls bobbed like they were in on the joke.

Forty minutes later, we descended the creaky wooden stairs of my family's old farmhouse, wafting vanilla-scented perfume with every step.

My dad did a double take on his way through the lounge to his office. "Nova, I thought you were Melody for a moment there. You look beautiful, darling. Ah… you too, Skye." He nodded somewhat awkwardly at her, I guess not sure if he should be complimenting the appearance of a teenage girl who wasn't his daughter, but not wanting her to feel left out.

"Thanks, Mr Samson," Skye said.

"Thanks, Dad." I couldn't help but smile. It was nice to be compared to my sister, Melody, who had an online fan base following her daily looks. Her style was ultra-feminine, modest, and beautiful, whereas my school uniform was usually the dressiest thing I wore.

After Skye had coaxed me into the dress that I owned in case of emergency weddings and baptisms, she'd done my makeup and then somehow curled my long brown hair with her straightening iron. I didn't quite understand how that worked, yet here we were.

For herself, Skye had chosen a nude, one-shoulder, wraparound dress that would have had me freaking out about security issues. It was something she didn't seem at all concerned about as we bustled into the kitchen to dump chips and pineapple lumps into bowls, and mix up punch. We had told the guys to arrive any time after 8pm, but so much time had been sucked up by my mini-makeover that 8pm was now only a couple of minutes away.

Mum sidled past where we were working and flicked on the jug. "Just making myself a cup of tea before I'm banished to my dungeon." She smiled cheekily at me, creases dimpling on either side of her mouth.

My parents had solemnly sworn they would stay out of sight for my birthday gathering, but they kept teasing me about it.

"Prisoners don't get tea," I snarled in a terrible impersonation of a prison warden from the olden days. "Ye will drink your tepid water and ye will like it."

Mum chuckled and finished making her drink before she drifted over towards me with her teacup in hand. I turned to face her in case she decided my birthday celebration was reason enough to hug me, but she merely smiled as she passed by and said, "Have a fun night with your friends."

"Thanks, Mum." I smiled back at her even as that all-too

familiar disappointment washed over me. I couldn't remember a time when Mum had hugged me without me initiating it first. And whenever I did hug her, she always squirmed out of it as quickly as she could. Covering my disappointment with a joke, I pointed to the doorway and said, "Now scram."

Mum exited the kitchen in the casually elegant way she did everything, jewellery jingling with each soft step. Skye and I followed shortly afterwards, carrying plentiful bowls of treats. We placed the snacks on various surfaces around my cosy lounge and then sank down onto the couch in front of the fireplace, sharing a bowl of pineapple lumps between us. Dad had lit the fire, more for atmosphere than warmth since the temperature was mild this far into spring.

"Soooo," Skye drawled as she pulled a cushion onto her lap. "Are you excited about tonight?"

"To be honest, I haven't really thought about it until now. Too busy studying." I popped a pineapple lump into my mouth.

"Oh yeah. It sucks how your birthday falls right before exams every year."

"I mean, it's not like I'll be sitting exams for the rest of my life... unless I royally botch them, I guess." Suddenly I felt terrified by that thought. "Oh man, why did I even think about failing? I *have* to pass. Did I tell you what Dad said?"

"No. What?" Skye raised her eyebrows.

"If I get an Excellence in accounting this year, he'll give me a part-time job at his work – in the accounts department. The pay would be pretty decent for high school. You and I might actually be able to take that trip to Bali after we graduate!"

"That's awesome! Go your dad! And, of course you'll get an Excellence." Skye patted my knee. "Your brain is amazing. Anyway, forgetting about exams for one beautiful night," Skye leaned her elbows on the cushion on her lap, "how do you feel about turning 17?"

"Good, I guess. I mean, how different will it really be from 16?"

"You know what...?" Skye cocked her head sideways and squinted at me like she was getting a message from above.

"What?" I asked, curious about what that look could mean.

"I have a feeling 17's going to be the year for you. I think you're officially coming into your own."

"Coming into my *what* now?" I scrunched my face.

"Coming into your own. I'm not totally sure what it means," she shrugged her freckled shoulders, "but I *think* it means that everyone is going to wake up to your innate awesomeness, or something like that."

"Well, I like the sound of that." I popped another pineapple lump into my mouth and tried to picture what the next year could bring. Skye did have a habit of foretelling the future. Not like a prophet or anything – more like she could just *will* events into happening. If she thought 17 was going to be the year for me, chances were, she'd make it happen. It obviously wouldn't involve love, but maybe other good things would come my way, like that job with my dad.

Hearing the doorbell, I sprang to my feet. It was party time. I smoothed down my dress and headed towards the tiled foyer, slipping around the corner to open our solid wood front door.

And there he was. Standing before me. Looking even more ridiculously handsome than ever in dress pants and a shirt knotted with a skinny tie. Andrew Tyler – Ty to his friends – raised his dark eyebrows as he took in my dressy appearance, but he didn't comment on it. Instead, he smiled crookedly and murmured, "Happy Birthday, Nova," before bending down to kiss my cheek and press a gift into my hands. I didn't breathe for the entire exchange.

Ty was my neighbour and oldest friend, so he had been at every one of my birthday parties. No matter the theme, his mother always insisted he wear a proper dress shirt, hand-deliver my present, and kiss me on my cheek. My mind flicked through a running montage of all these same-but-different birthday greetings over the years – Ty with his various haircuts ranging from short and orderly to its current state of unruly black.

"Thanks, Ty." I smiled, willing the breath back into my lungs as I looked up at him. He had overtaken me in height when we were thirteen and was now taller than me by half a head – something he definitely got from his dad's side of the family, just like I got my height from my dad. Taking a shaky step backwards, I gestured for him to come inside.

"Oh, is that Ty?" Skye squealed from the lounge. I didn't even hear her move, but suddenly she was sliding around the corner and jumping into his arms. She kissed him with a loud, theatrical, smacking sound before Ty lowered her to the ground and took her hand. Skye used it to pull him around the corner into the lounge.

They had got together a year ago, at my 16th birthday party. It was the night I'd finally realised my feelings for Ty, something that had previously been difficult for me to figure out because Skye's feelings for him were always so loud. We'd been eating dinner at an Italian restaurant in town, when Ty had winked at me and stolen a bite of my risotto. Everything had shifted for me in that instant. I'd watched Ty's lips close around my dinner and somehow felt them on my own lips.

It was a surreal night from that point on. I'd been in such a daze, completely caught up in my newly-discovered feelings for Ty as my friends and I wandered to an underage club on Karangahape Road. All five of us had danced together until our other two friends, Peter and Matthias, had gone to grab us a booth. When Skye had subtly flicked her fingers to gesture for me to sit down at the booth too, I'd instantly turned to leave. Ty had asked me to stay, but I'd smiled at him and Skye and told them to

have fun together, before leaving them alone on the dance floor.
Why did I leave them alone?

For so long I'd been Skye's wingman with Ty, to no avail, but even in that moment, when I'd just come to terms with my own feelings for Ty, I had automatically reverted to my best friend role and walked away. From the booth, I had watched Skye kiss Ty for the first time like the sparks were bullets through my own chest. As Skye had taken Ty's hand and pulled him back to our table, I'd made a decision: I would be happy for them, no matter what. I would never let either of them see my pain or even guess at my feelings.

So, when Skye had announced to everyone at the booth that she and Ty were going out, I'd smiled like I was the power source for *K* Road.

And for 364 days, I'd kept right on smiling.

I'd shoved my feelings down so deep; they rarely made an appearance. The only time I let myself think about what might have been was on my morning runs, when my angst transformed into motion. I came away from those runs clear-headed and able to set aside my wants for the benefit of my two best friends. It would ruin everything if either of them knew how I felt, so I never gave them the chance to suspect. It was my constant hope that one day I'd get over Ty and fall madly in love with someone I could actually be with.

This year, I'd organised my birthday party to be a day early so they could celebrate their one-year anniversary on the actual date. Even though Skye was amping for it, she had done her best to make my birthday party all about me. She was awesome like that.

As I trailed behind the happy couple into the lounge, I switched Ty's gift out for a bowl of salt and vinegar chips that was sitting on the ornate coffee table. "Chips?" I offered.

"Thanks!" Ty flashed his teeth, grabbing the bowl and

scooping up a handful of the potato chips. Skye rested her head against his left arm.

I looked away, off my game.

The doorbell rang again, and I was glad for the excuse to get away from their happiness and collect myself. Opening the front door once more, I was hit in the face by the odour of clashing male body sprays.

"Madame," Matthias Smith and Peter Liu said in tandem before flinging themselves into sweeping bows on my porch, wafting their formulated-in-a-can guy smells further my way. When they straightened back up to their full heights, Matthias stood a good foot taller than Peter. He was a bear of a guy, with small grey eyes that peered out from a broad ruddy face. Although Peter was shorter, he was just as muscly, thanks to the surfing we all did.

Before I could invite the boys inside, they launched into a weird hybrid mashup of *The Birthday Song* sung to the tune of *We Wish You a Merry Christmas*. They finished the song by falling dramatically to their knees and raising their arms to the sky, howling like wolves.

"That was beautiful." I pretended to wipe a tear off my cheek, then quickly ushered the boys inside before my neighbours poked their noses over the fence.

"Oh, wait!" Peter turned back around and headed for the porch, where he'd left a brightly-wrapped gift box. "This is for you," he said. "From both of us."

Murmuring my thanks, I took the present from him and carried it through to the lounge.

"Open it. Open it," Matthias began chanting in his deep voice as he followed me.

"Open it. Open it," Peter quickly took up the chant.

I couldn't help but grin at their enthusiasm as I took a seat on one of the blue velvet armchairs near the fire. Ripping off the wrapping paper, I found a plain cardboard box inside. It gave me no clues about what it contained, so I quickly jammed my nails into the seam to rip it open. Reaching inside, I pulled out a flat, round object that was a little bigger than my head. I almost dropped it when I saw what it was – an automated vacuum cleaner with an MP3 player docked into a wireless speaker on top.

"DJ *Roomba*!" I yelled, jumping to my feet with the robotic DJ in my hands. "This is so awesome!" I screeched again, jumping up and down in my excitement. "Thank you, guys." I barrelled into both of them for a group hug.

Matthias and Peter patted my back as Peter said, "I think she likes it."

"Like it?" I squeaked, stepping back. "I don't like it. I'm *obsessed* with it."

They had recreated DJ *Roomba* from our group's favourite TV show, *Parks and Recreation*. It was something only fans of the show would get, which made it next level.

"Thank you. Thank you. Thank you," I said as I stroked my gift.

"You're welcome." Peter grinned, his brown eyes crinkling around the edges. "I found the *Roomba* on *Trade Me* and – let's just say – I was inspired. Just be warned, it doesn't actually vacuum anymore, which is why I was able to nab it. These things usually run to a couple of grand, and, as much as I love you, I wasn't going to drop that kind of cash on your present."

"Well, my mum will probably be disappointed, but that actually makes it better," I said. "Now, she won't try and steal it from me."

While we'd been talking, Ty and Skye had jumped up from the couch to look at DJ *Roomba* too, so I passed it over to Skye to hold. She and Ty both cooed over it. Seriously, it was like having a celebrity in the house with us.

Matthias grabbed the *Roomba* off Ty and informed us, "I was in charge of your birthday playlist and it's a bop. Whaddya say we crank up DJ *Roomba* and get this party started?"

"Definitely." I nodded.

As Matthias turned on *Nova's 17th Birthday Party Mix* playlist, he showed me what he was doing so I'd know how to use it next time, and then he sent DJ *Roomba* rolling around the carpet. Ty hit the lights as the first song blared out from the speaker. It was *House of Pain's* "Jump Around," and switching it on seemed to flick on dance switches in all of us because we instantly began jumping and rapping badly in the firelight.

Skye leapt over to me and screamed happily over the loud music, "Best. Party. Ever!"

And in that moment, it really was.

CHAPTER

Two

I actually slept in on the morning after my party. Rare for me, since my body was used to waking up at 5am six days a week to go running, and never seemed to get the memo it could sleep a little later on Sundays. But we'd been having such a good time, no one had wanted to head home.

After our impromptu dance party, we'd played cards around the coffee table. I'd laughed so hard over all the smack talk that had gone down, my jaw had started to ache. The competition between Ty and Peter had been hilariously fierce.

Mum's voice cut through my memory-scape when she called to me from somewhere in the house, "Nova, we're leaving in thirty minutes. Are you coming?"

Detangling myself from my duvet so I could climb out of bed and open my bedroom door, I yelled back, "Yeah, I'll be down in a minute."

Last I'd heard, Skye was still planning to go to church before her anniversary date, so at least I'd get to briefly catch up with her before she and Ty had their day of joy.

Still half-asleep, I shuffled next door to the narrow bathroom I shared with my parents. I turned on the shower to let it warm up while I stripped off my PJs, then stepped into the tiled shower and closed the glass door behind me.

Unfortunately, I'd slept in for so long that I didn't have time to let the shower work its magic on my aching muscles. I ran the water just long enough to give my face and body a quick scrub, wishing I could bliss out for longer under the hot stream of water. I had been pushing myself in training all week, and my body felt it *everywhere*. The New Zealand Secondary Schools Track and Field Championships were in December – just two months away – and I was going to be one of the youngest long-distance runners in the senior division. I probably wouldn't even make it past the heats, but not for lack of training.

With a sad wrench, I turned off the shower and grabbed my towel from its heated rail. At least its warmth was a comfort as I wrapped it around my body.

Back in my minimalist white bedroom, I pulled on my favourite top with a pair of shorts. The top changed my eye colour from its usual murky sea blue to more of a sky blue. The curls had fallen out of my hair, and it was looking worse for wear after all that jumping around last night, so I just threw it up into its usual high ponytail and called it styled.

Grabbing my phone and purse, I went to find my parents so that I could catch a lift to church. Necessary, since I didn't have my own car yet. I found Mum and Dad out on the lawn next to our driveway, laughing over the scene they had discovered in our little kōwhai tree. There must have been a dozen tuis perched precariously on its thin branches, sucking vigorously at the yellow trumpet-shaped flowers that had suddenly bloomed all over it. The dark blue birds looked so funny with the white bobbles on their throats bouncing up and down as they gorged.

"They're having a good breakfast." I chuckled and pulled out my phone to snap a photo.

"It looks like an overloaded *Nickle Nackle Tree*." Dad laughed, and Mum giggled at his joke.

"That's exactly what it looks like." I smiled. "I can't believe the tree's holding up under all of their weight."

"Well, birds have hollow bones, you know? So they're very light." Dad loved passing on his knowledge to anyone who would listen. "In fact, their bones act as a second pair of lungs when they're flying, storing oxygen so they can travel long distances without getting tired. That's how they're able to migrate from one country to another. Isn't that amazing?"

"Actually, that is pretty cool," I agreed, thinking that I wouldn't mind having a secret store of oxygen for my long runs.

We watched the feasting tuis for a few moments longer, and then climbed into Dad's sedan to make the eight-minute drive to our little country church.

Skye was waiting for me in the foyer when we arrived.

"Happy Anniversary!" I squealed, throwing my arms around her shoulders. This was such a big day for her. Even though it was technically my birthday, her anniversary felt like the bigger deal.

"Thanks, Nova." Skye stepped out of my hug with a sweet-but-secretive smile, which had me cocking my head sideways at her curiously.

"Why are you looking so sly?" I asked.

"Ahhh..." She flicked her tongue over her slightly crossed-over front teeth, patted her canvas side-satchel, and said, "I bought something for today, but I need your opinion on it. Can I show it to you?"

"Of course you can," I reassured her.

"Not here!" She grabbed my hand and pulled me around the corner to the photocopy room, closing the door firmly behind us. Reaching into her side-satchel, Skye fished out a vivid red bikini – so red, it would have fit in nicely on the set of *Baywatch*.

"*Oi, Mama!*" I fanned my face jokingly. "That thing is flaming."

"I know, right?" Skye nodded enthusiastically. "I'm going to wear it under my wetsuit today so I can do a grand reveal after Ty and I finish surfing. I'm pretty sure he'll die when he sees it."

"Die, or adjust the waistband of his boardies uncomfortably. You really want to inflict all this on him?" I waved my hand over her toned and perky body to indicate what *all this* meant.

"It's not about torturing him, I swear," she replied, inspecting the bikini again. "But a year's a long time to be together without doing the deed. I want to remind him exactly what he's waiting for."

"Uh, I'm pretty sure he *knoooows.*"

Ty was Catholic and on board with the whole idea of saving sex for the marriage bed, but that didn't make it easy – for either of them. I had the joy of hearing about it from Skye. All. The. Time. Luckily, Ty never discussed his private relationship with me. Thank goodness for small mercies.

"It's a balancing act, ya know?" Skye held out her hands like a set of scales, with the bikini in one hand and nothing in the other. "Keeping the attraction alive without going too far. Lately it feels like we've been more friend-zone than boyfriend/girlfriend, and I thought the bikini might help spice things up."

"Fair enough." I nodded sagely, as if I was in any position to give her relationship advice. "That bikini will do it."

"Anyway, the only thing I'm actually worried about is if the bikini's going to shift around while I'm surfing and give Ty a *way* bigger show than I want." Skye widened her eyes in mock-horror. "I need a second opinion. Is this going to hold up under my wetsuit or not?"

I took the bikini from her and hot-potatoed it back and forth between my hands like it was burning me. "Hot. Hot. Hot," I gasped with each toss.

Skye groaned at my antics but then grinned, displaying her cutely crooked front teeth for me again.

Winking at her, I made a show of unfurling her bikini to

examine it, even though I already knew it would be fine. Skye, Ty, and I had all started surfing lessons when we were ten-year-old grommets, and, after losing my bikini top in the water one summer, I'd built up an accurate score system of the best togs to surf in: Crossover *Speedo* one-pieces were a solid ten out of ten; string bikinis should be burned at the stake. This bikini fell somewhere in the middle. "Clasps look solid and the cut's good," I told Skye. "I think you'll be safe."

"I thought as much, but figured you'd steer me clear if there was any danger. You've been so paranoid ever since The Great Bikini Incident."

"I'm seriously never going to live that down," I grumbled, handing the bikini back to her.

"You're just lucky nobody had their phones in the water with them, or we'd all be reliving that experience with you on *YouTube*."

"Moving right along...." I rolled my eyes and my hands simultaneously. "Apart from surfing, do you know what else Ty's got planned for you tonight?"

"Nope. He won't share the deets. Although, I think the whole thing's happening out at Piha because he told me to bring warm clothes to change into after surfing."

"It's going to be so good. Promise me you'll take heaps of photos so I can live vicariously through you," I said, hating myself a little for meaning it. Vicarious was as good as it got for me.

"I will," Skye assured me. "I'll snap the whole night for you."

Just then, our worship band started playing in the church hall, so Skye shoved her bikini back into her side-satchel, and the two of us headed for our seats.

CHAPTER
Three

Skye was true to her word about sharing photos, and it looked like she was having the best anniversary date imaginable.

I lay on the couch after dinner, scrolling through her photo feed while watching a cheesy girls' night out movie with Mum. Our tabby cat, Mr Fluffy Pants, was stretched out on my hip, his front paws reaching towards me like he was dreaming about flying.

Mum perched primly on the armchair closest to the fire. It was her favourite spot since she always felt the cold – and because she didn't have to share it with anyone.

Skye had already posted a string of photos of her and Ty at the beach. In all the photos, Skye's hair billowed out wildly around her head like a lion's mane while her scorching red bikini held everything together superbly. Ty's windblown black hair was doing something similarly lionesque after his surf, and he'd stripped down to bronze boardies that were only a shade or two darker than his skin. Skye and Ty's eyes sparkled in the setting sun as they stood with their arms wrapped around each other looking like models for… pretty much anything good in this world.

As the night progressed, Skye had added more pics of the two of them bundled up and picnicking on Lion Rock in the dark. She had posted the last photo about 30 minutes ago, and it was a beautiful side-on shot of Ty looking up at the stars, his expression wondrous.

Mum sighed from her armchair. I glanced over and noticed her cringing at a swear word on the movie we were half-heartedly watching.

"You okay there, Ma?" I asked her.

"I'm not sure I can take much more of this, Nova." Mum grimaced, pulling on her silver bob as if to block her ears. "That's the third vulgar word I've heard tonight."

Finding a movie my conservative 60-year-old mother and I both enjoyed was pretty much impossible, but Mum had wanted to do something to celebrate my birthday with me. We'd compromised with a movie neither of us wanted to watch.

"The movie's pretty rubbish." I clicked off the TV and shifted Mr Fluffy Pants off me so I could stand up. "I think I'll head to bed."

"Oh! Are you sure?" The worry lines on Mum's soft face deepened. "Don't turn it off on my account. You're the birthday girl."

"Nah, that's cool," I replied. "Early start and all that. G'night." I lifted my hand in farewell and headed for the staircase. Mum got up to follow me.

Since my alarm was always set for 5am during the week, I should've been in bed already, but I'd masochistically stayed awake to watch the anniversary photos roll in. This vulgar swearing-on-the-movie thing had actually worked out great for me. I needed to let Ty and Skye enjoy their lives and move on with my own, which started with me getting a good night's sleep.

I headed upstairs to wash my face and brush my teeth. Hearing a ping from the phone in my pocket, I quickly scrubbed my face dry and scooped out my phone. The message was from Skye.

Skye: *I need to talk to you.*

Weird to be hearing from her tonight, when she was still on her anniversary date, but I texted back, *"What about?"* and then waited for her reply as I headed back to my bedroom.

It was a few minutes later when my phone pinged again. I swiped the screen to read it, but saw that this message was from Ty instead.

Ty: *Help! We just crashed and Skye's not moving. I'm freaking out.*

The room around me started to contract and expand. I had to sit down on my bed because I suddenly understood fear like I never had before. It reached in and grabbed my stomach with a hard jerk, leaving me sick and breathless.

With shaking fingers, I texted Ty back: *What? Have you called 111?*

And then I struggled to breathe as I waited for his response to come through. When it finally did, the chime of my phone shot adrenaline directly into my heart.

Ty: *Not me. Someone else has. A passer-by.*

I texted him back immediately: *Are you okay?*

No response.

No response.

No response.

My entire body felt jittery and sick as I waited for him to reply, but he didn't, and I couldn't sit there doing nothing for a second longer.

Skye's not moving.

Leaping off my bed, I sprinted down the hall to my parents' bedroom, crashing into their door as I fumbled to open it with clammy hands. Dad muttered something about privacy as I launched into their room, but then jerked to a stop when he saw the expression on my face.

Skye's not moving.

"What is it, Nova?" he asked, scanning me.

Tears must have been pouring down my face because Dad closed the gap between us and threw his arms around me while Mum moved closer and kneaded her hands together fretfully.

By now I was seriously choking back sobs, so it was hard to get the words out, but I finally managed to say, "Ty and Skye have been in a car accident. I don't know much, but Ty said Skye isn't moving."

"Noooo!" Mum gasped, and that simple word exactly encapsulated all the agony and powerlessness I was feeling.

"What can we do?" I urgently whipped my head back and forth between Mum and Dad, searching for something. Anything.

Their faces did *not* reassure me. My parents looked as lost as I felt, until Dad said, "I guess the best thing we can do right now is pray."

I nodded in a haze, and the three of us climbed onto Mum and Dad's enormous sleigh-style bed and huddled together, thanking God for my friends and *begging* him to bring them safely through this. "You're the one who created the entire universe. You created my friends," I acknowledged. "Please save Skye. Don't take her yet. Please God."

Mum and Dad kept praying long past the point where I had curled up into a catatonic ball. A text from Ty pulled me back to sitting fifteen minutes after his first one had come through: *We're in an ambulance on our way to Waitakere Hospital. Skye's getting CPR.*

My parents began praying again with renewed vigour after that, but I didn't join them this time. I was too busy racing to my room to get dressed so I could go to the hospital too. Action was exactly what I needed.

I threw on the exercise clothes I'd been planning to wear for my morning run, crammed my feet into my sneakers, and then dashed back to my parents' room.

"Can one of you please drive me to the hospital?" I asked, hopping from foot to foot. I only had my restricted licence, so I wasn't allowed to drive after 10pm. It probably wasn't safe for me to drive anyway, distraught as I was.

Skye's not moving.

"I'll take you," Dad volunteered. "Do you want to come, Serena?" He turned towards Mum to ask her.

"No." She shook her head, looking unusually frazzled for Mum, like a porcelain doll that's been roughed up after years of standing sweetly on a stand. "I'll get the prayer chain onto this and keep praying from here."

"Thanks, Mum." I said, before urging Dad, "Let's go. Let's go!"

Dad had to change out of his pyjamas, so that took a few more minutes, which felt like centuries, but finally we were seated side by side in his sedan, driving to the hospital. Sitting there, dark and enclosed, it felt like we were in a portal outside of time. Surely everything was going to be okay. Surely Ty's next message would tell me Skye had woken up and was going to be just fine.

But we weren't even halfway to the hospital when Ty's fourth and final text of the night blasted through my serenity: *She's gone. I'm so sorry Nova.*

CHAPTER

Four

It was the end of everything good.

By the time we got to the hospital, I was sobbing so violently that the triage nurse had to come and sit with me in the waiting room while Dad talked to the receptionist. I didn't know if that was the normal protocol for triage nurses, but some still-aware part of me appreciated her for it.

Unfortunately, the receptionist told Dad we weren't allowed to see Skye and that almost broke me. Dad took over from the triage nurse as my chief comforter, and I cried a wet patch into the shoulder of his *Polo* shirt while we waited for Ty to finish getting treated.

Dad's shoulder, solid as it was, provided no escape from my thoughts or my pain. Skye was dead. Gone for good. I'd never hear her voice again. Never hug her, or talk with her, or laugh with her. Never sing, or play, or share this life with her again. The only thing left to do was say goodbye. She'd already moved on. Our story was done with a cold brutality that left me reeling.

It couldn't be true. None of this could be true. If I could just see her, maybe I would believe she was really gone. Not that I wanted to believe it. I wanted to curl away from the knowledge that she was dead forever, but it kept whipping me in the chest like an electric cord.

Skye's dead. *Crack.*

She's gone. *Crack.*

I'm never going to see her again. *Crack.*

Dad rubbed my back as I sobbed over the girl who had been my best friend for almost a decade.

By the time Rosamie and James Tyler walked their son around the corner from one of the treatment rooms, my mouth had grown parched and my nose was raw from constant blowing.

Dad and I both leapt to our feet as soon as we saw the Tylers, which drew their gazes our way.

I scanned Ty from head to foot, checking him for damage. He had a bandage on his chin and his eyes were glazed, but, other than that, he seemed fine.

Rosamie, Ty's tiny Filipino mother, started crying softly when we walked up to them. Her much taller *Pākehā* husband, James, put his arm around her to comfort her, but directed his words our way when he said: "Andrew's being discharged. He had to get stitches on his chin, and the doctor sedated him to calm him down, but other than that, he's fine. Well... not fine, obviously..." James shrugged a tear off his cheek with the shoulder of his arm that was wrapped around Rosamie.

Ty stood on the other side of his dad but was staring at his feet, not engaging in the conversation at all.

"Have you seen Skye?" I asked his parents.

"No," Rosamie replied with a hitch to her breathing. "They wouldn't let us see her, but her family is with her."

I should've felt relieved that Skye wasn't alone, but all I felt was disappointment that *we* couldn't be with her. Ty and I may not have been blood relatives, but we were as close to Skye as family. Maybe closer. We were the family she had chosen.

James and Rosamie left Ty with us as they went to the reception to ask if there was anything more they needed to do before taking Ty home. I took the opportunity to talk to Ty, dazed as he was.

"Can I hug you?" I asked. "Or are you too sore?"

"Hug away," he replied flatly.

It was weird to see him so emotionless, but I could tell by his swollen eyes that he had been crying before the sedative had kicked in. I stretched up to slide my arms around his broad shoulders. Ty wrapped his arms around my back, but his fingers got caught in my hair because I'd forgotten to tie it back in my rush to get to the hospital. Untangling himself, Ty stroked my hair down the length of my back.

"Thank God you're okay." I squeezed him tightly, reassuring myself that he was still here at least and not about to disappear on me.

"Skye's not." His breath was a whisper on my neck. "I can't believe I killed her. It's my fault she's gone."

"Oh, Ty," I moaned into his broad shoulder, which smelled like a combination of sea salt and antiseptic. "Please don't blame yourself. It was an accident."

"But if I'd been more careful, it never would have happened," he insisted. "It *is* my fault."

Ty was a naturally cautious driver, and I knew he'd never risk hurting Skye, so I said, "I don't blame you, and I'm sure nobody else will either."

"I can't believe this has happened," he mumbled into my hair.

I *hated* that he was in pain. Stepping back so I could squeeze his hands and make eye contact with him, I tried again to reassure him. "You're going to be okay. You'll see. You'll get through this."

As soon as I said it, I recognised it for the false comfort it was because there was no way *I* was going to be okay, and I hadn't been the one dating Skye for the past year, or the one driving the car that had killed her.

"We'll get through this," I said, even though my entire body ached with unspent grief.

CHAPTER

Five

My tinkling phone alarm had me rearing out of bed at 5am the next morning. I'd forgotten to unset it.

Skye's dead.

That knowledge barrelled into me stronger than any West Coast wave ever had. I angrily tapped at my screen to turn off the alarm. There was no chance I'd fall back asleep now, despite having cried myself to sleep well after midnight. Already the tears were pouring in such a continuous stream down my face that my nose started running too, and I had to grab tissue after tissue to clear it. Grief felt like the worst kind of sickness – my nose ran, and my lungs squeezed uncomfortably tight in my chest. Meanwhile, my stomach heaved like it wanted to throw up.

Skye...

I longed to call her and hear her voice, to reassure myself this was nothing more than a bad dream. Skye couldn't be dead. Things like that didn't just happen. Or they shouldn't. Wasn't it just yesterday she'd been showing me her hot red bikini, all nervously excited about her anniversary with Ty? Today, she was lying in a morgue. And then it hit me – she'd died on my birthday. How was I supposed to celebrate that ever again? How was I supposed to celebrate *anything* ever again, without my best friend by my side?

I guess she'd been wrong about 17 being my best year yet.

I started gasping at the unfairness of it all. I couldn't handle it. I wasn't equipped to handle this kind of pain. Yet somehow, I had to find a way to do exactly that. How did people live with grief like this?

Running was the only thing I could think of that might temporarily distance my mind from the pain. It had always numbed my thoughts in the past, so maybe it could offer me relief in this too – the worst morning of my life.

Slipping into my fluorescent running shoes, I made my way downstairs and out the front door. I was still wearing the same exercise clothes I'd worn to the hospital the night before – a lifetime ago – but at least I was ready to run.

I tore madly down our rickety farmhouse steps and onto our quiet country cul-de-sac, which led downhill to its intersection with Laingholm Drive. Checking for cars, I sprinted across the road to the side with the footpath and then turned right to head up the hill in the direction of the beach. I took that hill faster than I ever had before, faster than was sensible, but I had to do something with the maelstrom of panic and pain whirling inside me.

Running eased the burning in my chest to something bearable, and I would have gladly kept going forever, but by the time I'd made it up over the hump of the tree-covered hill and back down to the beach, I'd used up every drop of energy I had. I sagged onto a wooden bench facing the sea, and that's when it hit me again like it was fresh news… Skye was dead. My best friend was no more, and I was bereft. I fell sideways on the bench and curled up into a ball as the agony of Skye's death tore through me all over again.

So many plans gone in an instant. A whole life imagined… turned imaginary. The tears didn't so much pour out of me as explode. Great racking sobs that felt like they might crack my ribs in two. I curled deeper into myself and failed miserably to hold my straining chest together. Life shouldn't be such a flimsy thing, so weakly tethered to this earth. What was the point of making plans when they could all be turned to dust in an instant?

After eventually crying myself out, I stood up and dazedly stretched my cramped muscles, barely noticing the flat sea view in front of me before I staggered back home in a body that had become a stranger to me.

Mum and Dad were soberly preparing breakfast in the kitchen when I came limping through the front door of our old farmhouse. One look at their pitying faces and I knew I couldn't stick around, or we'd all be in for a repeat of the bench scene. I fled upstairs to my bathroom to shower, where I thirstily drank water straight from the shower head and then washed the tears off my salt-worn face in disbelief. How could Skye be dead? How? And, more baffling, how was I supposed to go on living now that she was gone?

It occurred to me that there was only one other person who would truly understand what I'd lost.

After showering and throwing on a t-shirt and track pants, I slipped back out of my house and across the road to Ty's house. It was a lot newer than ours, built when the original section across the street had been subdivided two decades before. It had always felt like a refuge to me, backing peacefully onto a native bush reserve the way it did; full of people I adored. Hopefully, that sense of refuge would extend even to today.

Reaching the Tylers' front door, I opened it and called out a soft, "Hello." I'd stopped knocking years ago, at Rosamie's insistence. "Our home is your home, baby girl," she always said.

Rosamie must have heard my *hello* from the kitchen because she rushed over to wrap her short arms around me.

"How are you doing, Nova Pie?" she asked from somewhere around my ribs.

I couldn't even answer her. I just hugged her back and tried not to cry into her glossy black hair, which smelled like a combination of vanilla and jasmine.

"I know, baby girl," she murmured. "I know. You just let it out."

So, I did. Again. After my tears eventually tapered out, Rosamie stepped back and said, "Andrew is still asleep, but you're welcome to eat *champorado* with me."

"Yes, please." I smiled through my tears. "That sounds like the perfect kind of comfort food right now."

Champorado was this heavenly Filipino chocolate rice porridge that Rosamie made several mornings a week for breakfast. I had never been able to resist it, in all my seventeen years of neighbourly visits. I'm pretty sure it was the food I'd weaned off breast milk onto.

Rosamie squeezed my arm once before turning around and leading the way through her plant-filled lounge into her kitchen. Once there, she dolloped a huge serving into a bowl for me.

"Thank you so much." I carried it to the rimu dining table to eat, grabbing a spoon off the servery on my way.

Rosamie joined me with her own bowl moments later and said grace. I copied her in making the sign of the cross as she said, "In the name of the Father, the Son, and the Holy Ghost. Amen." It was something her family always did, and I'd picked up on it early in life. On that particular morning, it helped remind me that although the worst may have happened, God still remained.

"So, how's Ty doing? Really?" I asked before taking my first sweet mouthful of the rice porridge.

"I'm not sure," Rosamie sighed, lifting her round shoulders and dropping them again heavily. She looked tired. And worried. "He was already sedated when we got to the hospital last night, and he fell asleep as soon as we got home. He must have been out of his mind with grief if they had to sedate him. He's normally such a calm boy."

"Yeah," I agreed softly. Even with the drugs, I could tell the grief and guilt were eating at him when we'd spoken last night. "Did he tell you what happened? How they crashed?"

"All he told us was that one minute they were driving along Scenic Drive, talking, the next they were sliding into a tree. It happened on a corner, so I guess he took it too fast?" she said that last part with a questioning inflection. "The police did a blood test, which came up clear of course, but he might lose his licence anyway."

"Oh no!" I exclaimed. "I hope he doesn't." Ty had only got his full licence a few weeks ago – the second person in our group of school friends to get it, after Peter. He had done a defensive driving course so he could get it before he turned eighteen. I was doing the same course, but since I was six months younger than Ty, I still wasn't eligible to sit the test. "I guess his car's written off anyway?"

"Yes," she sighed. "Well and truly. Although we don't care about that. We'd gladly lose the car if we could have Skye back."

"Yeah, I'd give anything to have Skye back again." I pressed my lips together and looked at Rosamie helplessly as tears began their inevitable descent down my cheeks.

Rosamie reached across the table and squeezed my hand as her own tears began falling. We managed to eat the rest of our breakfast one-handed and in silence, two lambs lost in the wilderness, eating because we didn't know what else to do.

After scraping the bowl clean and swallowing my last mouthful, I retracted my hand from Rosamie so I could wipe my eyes and say, "Thank you for breakfast. It was exactly what I needed. Would it be okay if I went and sat with Ty for a bit? I promise I won't wake him. I just need to reassure myself he's okay."

"Of course, darling girl." She nodded, taking my bowl and

spoon and stacking them with her own on the table to let me know I was free to go. "You've always been such a good friend to him. He needs that right now, more than ever."

Rising to my feet, I thanked her again and headed down the hallway past a painting of *The Blessed Virgin Mary* towards Ty's bedroom. His door was slightly ajar, like Rosamie had already peeked in on him that morning. I eased it open all the way and found Ty lying on his stomach in the middle of his queen-sized bed. He had his arms tucked under his pillow in his favourite sleeping position – the one I remembered from countless camping trips when we were kids. As softly as I could, I walked over to his bed and sat down next to him, leaning my back against his sage-painted wall.

Just smelling his familiar scent and watching him breathe helped to settle me. What if I'd lost him too? I really could have. Both of my best friends could've been taken in a split second. I shuddered just thinking about it. It was already too much to bear, losing Skye; I couldn't imagine saying goodbye to *both* of them. I felt guilty for even thinking it, but thank God Ty had survived.

It was obvious when Ty woke up because he began sniffing into his pillow. I grabbed the tissue box off his rimu side table and pushed it towards him. Tissues were going to be our constant companions for a while, I could tell. Ty curled onto his side to blow his nose, and then threw the tissue in the general vicinity of his rubbish bin before inching towards me and laying his head on my lap. He was still crying with his eyes closed.

I stroked his messy black hair while he wrung himself out, my own tears falling softly as I ached for Skye: Her enthusiasm; Her energy; Her joyful zest for life; Her drive and determination. Everything that made her who she was had been wiped out from this world, from *my* world. I could almost see the gap she'd left behind. She should've been *right there* in Ty's room with us, but she wasn't.

Time lost all meaning for me as Ty cried, but eventually his sobs tapered off into an occasional shudder, and then he murmured something too soft for me to catch.

"What was that?" I leaned down to hear him better.

Ty turned his head and looked up at me for the first time that morning. His eyes were red-rimmed. My own eyes immediately snagged on the bandage on his chin – the only physical reminder he'd been in a fatal car accident the night before.

"I'm so glad you're here," he said again, audibly this time.

"Me too."

We both must've been clinging hard to the fact we still had each other – our only comfort in a comfortless time. I stroked his hair again as the tears began rolling more fervently down my face. "I keep thinking, what if you'd died too? I could have lost you both."

"Maybe that would've been better," he mumbled so quietly, it was like he hadn't meant for me to hear.

"Don't say that," I gasped, grabbing his shoulders as if that would keep him tethered to this life with me. "Don't *ever* say that. I am in agony over Skye's death, and you *not* dying is the only thing getting me through this."

"Okaay," he breathed, and I removed my hands from his shoulders, but the dam had broken on my tears, which were rapidly turning into sobs as I longed for Skye to return to us with all of my broken heart.

Now it was Ty's turn to hold me as I cried. He climbed up onto his knees and wrapped his arms around me. I fell into him and sobbed until the shoulder of his t-shirt was soaked through, but he didn't complain, and he didn't let go. The sense of well-being that washed over me as I knelt in his embrace was one I couldn't remember ever experiencing before. I was so rarely held by anyone. Although Skye's death had ripped me in two, Ty's strong and familiar arms around me were working to temporarily stitch me back together.

The thing that eventually pulled us apart was the very practical need for the tissue box. We both blew our noses to clear them as best we could and then sank exhaustedly down onto Ty's bed and fell asleep.

CHAPTER

Six

Rosamie's softly accented voice woke us from our slumber. "Andrew. Nova. I've made you *sinangag* for lunch," she said, which caused me to register the garlicky smell of her signature fried rice at the same time as I realised that Ty was curled into my back.

Rosamie blinked at us as she held out a wooden tray carrying two bowls. I quickly shifted away from Ty and sat up, not wanting her to get the wrong idea about the nature of us being in bed together.

"Thank you, Rosamie," I said, falling back on manners to smooth over the awkward situation.

Ty didn't appear discomfited at all as he cleared his throat next to me and asked in a gravelly voice, "Could I please have a drink of water, Mum?"

"Of course." Rosamie set the wooden tray down on the side table next to him and exited the bedroom. She returned with two tall glasses, one for each of us.

"Thank you, Rosamie," I said again, still feeling sheepish about the way she'd found us in bed together, but continuing to act normal so she wouldn't make a big deal out of it. "This is so kind of you."

"Yeah. Thanks, *Nanay*," Ty used the informal Filipino

endearment for *Mum*, which slipped out from time to time. He dug into his sinangag, and I realised it was his first meal of the day, so he was probably ravenous.

"Anything for my darlings." Rosamie smiled, and I felt relieved she wasn't going to ask us unnecessary questions. "Let me know if you need anything else," she said before leaving us alone again – with the door wide open.

Ty finished his food before I'd even got through half of mine, and I noticed him eyeing up my bowl longingly. I was still full from my breakfast, so I offered the rest to him.

"You're the best." He smiled his thanks, but it quickly teetered into a grimace as I saw the guilt wash through him again. How was he ever going to come to terms with the fact he'd accidentally killed his girlfriend? I couldn't even begin to imagine what that process would entail.

Since I couldn't think of any wise words of comfort, I just smoothed his unruly hair with my hand and said, "I'm going to go and use the bathroom. I'll be back soon."

He nudged my hand with his head like a cat begging to be stroked, so I spent a few seconds scratching the top of his scalp before heading off to use the toilet. As long as I'd known him, Ty had loved getting his head scratched.

When I returned from the bathroom, Ty had finished my lunch and needed to use the toilet too. He went off to do his business while I crawled back into his bed. Although my grief over Skye was all-encompassing, I felt safe being there with Ty, like we'd been given this brief reprieve when nothing else bad could touch us.

I must have drifted back to sleep because I woke to the bed shifting under me as Ty climbed back in. He was freshly showered and wearing an old running shirt and track pants. The bandage on his chin was damp and seeping a bit with blood.

"Do you want me to change that?" I asked him.

"Yeah. Thanks." He climbed back out of bed and walked over to his tallboy where a stash of hospital grade bandages was piled on top.

I got up and followed him, looking over the supplies and figuring out what I needed to use. As gently as possible, I peeled off the tape that secured the dressing to his chin. Ty winced but didn't complain. Once the tape was off, I could see the cut across the bottom of his chin where it was held together by stitches and steri-strips. The skin around it had started to turn purple with bruising, even as dark stubble peeked through the contusion.

Using my best wound care knowledge, I replaced the bandage with a sterile one and taped it into place. Ty watched me work through lowered lashes and then pulled me in for a one-armed hug when I'd finished patching him up.

"Thank you," he murmured into the side of my head. "You make everything better."

"Ditto," I replied.

"Hey, I had an idea while I was in the shower," Ty said, walking backwards a couple of steps to sit down on his bed.

"Yeah?" I tilted my head to the side, leaning back against his tallboy. "What was it?"

"I was thinking…," he hesitated, "do you want to take the Eucharist with me?"

"Do you mean like Communion?" I asked. Since I went to a Baptist church and Ty went to a Catholic one, we had different names for pretty much the same thing.

"Yeah." Ty nodded, leaning his elbows on his muscular thighs. "My head is full-on spinning over Skye being gone, and I feel so guilty about it," he sighed. "I think it would be good to take a moment to put everything into perspective and remember that God has a plan, even now, when it feels like I'm living an actual nightmare. When I was in the shower, I had this picture of Jesus taking the last supper before he was crucified, and I remembered that without him making that covenant with us, there wouldn't have been any hope for Skye when she died last night. And I know it feels like no kind of consolation right now, when all we want is Skye back, but that's why I think it's important we do this, otherwise we might let this tear us away from God."

I had never heard Ty speak so passionately about his faith like this before. Wanting to encourage him, I said, "I love that idea. I'll definitely take the Eucharist with you."

Ty pulled himself back to his feet and said, "Thank you. I'll go get the stuff." He grabbed the tray with our empty bowls and glasses on it and carried it out of the room.

While he was gone, I made myself comfy on his bed again, leaning against a pillow propped up by the wall behind me. The pillow smelled like Ty, and that comforted me.

When Ty came back, he still had the tray, but this time it held a bottle of Pinot Noir and a couple of rice crackers.

With reverence, Ty set the tray on my lap and then climbed onto the bed beside me, propping up a pillow behind him too. He picked up the rice crackers and held one out to me, repeating the words Jesus had spoken at the last meal he'd eaten before dying, "Take this and eat of it: for this is my body which will be given up for you."

We both ate our crackers with our eyes closed, and I don't know what Ty was thinking about, but I pictured Skye meeting Jesus in the flesh for the first time. I could practically see their radiant smiles and it helped ease the pain in my heart a little bit.

When our chewing had tapered off, Ty picked up the bottle of wine and twisted off the lid. Its rich aroma filled my nostrils. Holding the bottle out to me, Ty once again echoed Jesus as he said, "Take this and drink from it: for this is the chalice of my blood, the blood of the new and eternal covenant, which will be poured out for you and for many for the forgiveness of sins. Do this in memory of me."

I took a swig of the wine and then wiped the rim of the bottle with my shirt before passing it back to Ty. As he took his sip, I prayed a simple prayer – thanking Jesus for saving me and asking for God's comfort to fill everyone who was grieving over Skye. Just as I'd finished praying, a knock on Ty's bedroom door had me looking up.

Peter and Matthias were standing in the doorway, wearing school uniforms on their bodies and tears on their cheeks.

"I just can't believe it." Matthias shook his head as he came lumbering towards us. "I mean, is this real? It can't be real. Is Skye really dead? They told us at school that she is, but it doesn't feel real. Is it real?"

I squirmed as I realised neither Ty nor I had told the boys what had happened to Skye. How awful for them to find out at school.

Matthias's thoughts seemed to be spiralling around a rabbit hole of disbelief and grief, so I patted the bed on the other side of me from Ty, indicating that he should hop on beside me. The bed sagged as he did, sending me rolling towards him, but I shifted closer to Ty to give Matthias space.

And then I glanced up at Peter, who still stood uncertainly in the doorway while tears streamed down his cheeks. I held out my arms to him and he immediately crawled onto the bed and collapsed into my lap.

Just like that, we were all full-blown crying. We wept and hugged each other, passing the tissue box around and biting our lips as the shock of Skye's death rolled through us all once more.

The peace of the Eucharist was shattered. Death sucked.

CHAPTER

Seven

My sleep that night was broken by nightmares of Skye walking away without saying goodbye. Waking was no relief as the nightmare continued to stalk me.

It was a relief when my alarm went off at 5am on Tuesday morning, giving me a reason to get out of bed and go running. The repetitive motion of my feet hitting the concrete soothed me, and I threw myself into the run without holding anything back. I then staggered home to shower and throw on the snuggliest outfit I owned – a Minion onesie I'd worn to Peter's costume party last year. I was seeking solace in any form I could get it.

My youngest older sister, Melody, slipped into the house while I was eating a breakfast of *Vogel's* toast and *Marmite*. She had twined her cinnamon hair into a braid-bun thing and wore a sheer blouse over a camisole and high-waisted black pencil skirt. Judging by the formality of her outfit, she'd meant to head to work that morning but had somehow ended up here instead.

"Oh! My baby!" She wailed when she saw me. "Oh! My sweetheart! How are you holding up?" She yanked me into a strongly-perfumed hug. I went with it, resting my head on her shoulder and letting her coo over me.

Melody was 10 years older than me. My other sisters,

Gretchen and Veronica, were 12 and 14 years older than me, respectively. I'd been the classic surprise baby, arriving a decade after Mum and Dad had thought their family was complete. It meant my sisters had all acted like mini mothers towards me, often more so than my actual mother, who had been depressed for a lot of my childhood and hadn't seemed to want me there.

"There, there." Melody rubbed my back soothingly, as if I was crying, which I wasn't. My run had tired me out so much, I felt numb.

Eventually, I managed to extricate myself from Melody's grip and ask, "Aren't you supposed to be at work?"

"I took bereavement leave." Melody shrugged, like that was self-explanatory.

"But you're not related to Skye," I pointed out.

"Technicalities." Melody waved that away with a flick of her manicured hand. "I'm here for you; whatever you need. What *do* you need?"

"I don't know." I looked around our dining room wildly, hoping an idea would jump out at me.

"Well, you're clearly not going to school any time soon," she said firmly, "so, do you want me to run you a bubble bath?"

"No, I just showered."

"Perfect. You don't want to be soaking in your own filth anyway. Bubble baths are about self-care and giving you space to be with your thoughts, not cleanliness. I'll get it started." And with that, she traipsed along the hallway on legs almost as long as mine to run me a bath in our large downstairs bathroom.

The bath turned out to be perfect. It was deep and frothy, and Melody had set up a wireless speaker on the bathroom vanity so I could listen to soothing music while I soaked. The water wrapped around me like comforting arms, and I stayed in its warm embrace for more than an hour, adding hot water to continue the illusion that I wasn't so desperately alone. The steaming water felt especially delicious against all the muscles I'd overworked in my mad morning marathons.

When I finally emerged from the bathroom and headed upstairs to my bedroom, I found Melody perched like a leggy heron on my bed next to my next oldest sister, Gretchen.

"Nova Pie!" Gretchen jumped up and scrunched her fingers in a grabby gesture. I didn't even see her move, but suddenly she was pulling me in for a hug, despite the fact I was only wearing a mid-sized towel and her head was eye level with my breasts.

"Hey, Gretch," I said into the top of her dark bob, clawing my towel against my chest with my left hand. At just a couple of inches past five foot, Gretchen was way shorter than the rest of us sisters. She took after Mum in that respect. We often teased her about being the runt of the litter. Runt or not, she had definitely been endowed with more curves than me.

"Get dressed, my darling," she ordered me. "Melody and I are taking you out."

"Oh no." I backed away from her, spraying drops of water as I shook my head. "You don't need to do that. Really."

"Yes," Gretchen insisted, her hazel eyes flashing with determination. "We do. You've lost your best friend. Your life's been turned upside down. Let us take care of your needs. It's the least we can do."

"What *needs* are we talking about exactly?" I asked, edging away from my suddenly suffocating sisters towards my wardrobe. As kind as they were trying to be, their presence just reminded me of why I'd loved Skye so much. She had never babied me the way my sisters did. Never acted like I was too precious to try something dangerous. She'd been the one to encourage me into the male-dominated sports of surfing and rugby when we were kids. Later, I had switched from rugby to long-distance running, when I had realised my build was better suited to it, but I might not have tried any of it without Skye urging me on.

I had to hold in a sob so I could concentrate on what Melody was saying: "We're thinking this would be a good day for self-care. Clearly, none of us are going to be able to wear mascara to the funeral, so why don't we go and get our eyelashes tinted together?"

"Okay," I said. "That doesn't sound too bad."

"And do you have anything to wear to the funeral?" Gretchen asked me.

"Ummm, not really." All I wanted to wrap myself in these days were comfy oversized clothes.

"Maybe we could look for something while we're out then," Melody said.

"Sure," I agreed. I guess a yellow onesie wouldn't really communicate the respect I felt for my friend and her funeral.

Melody made us appointments with her beauty therapist in Newmarket and drove us there in her dinky little *Suzuki Swift*. As soon as we pulled open the door of the beauty clinic, the inviting aroma of rose and cardamom wafted out to greet us. Inside, candles lit the foyer and soft music played from a discrete speaker, giving the space a restful vibe.

A shiny-skinned receptionist greeted us and took us through to a cosy back room where a beauty therapist called Claire tinted our eyelashes. It didn't make any noticeable improvement to my eyes, which were so swollen from crying I was shocked Claire could even find my eyelashes. Still, it was nice to feel cared for in this way.

After we finished up there, we wandered Broadway looking for a muted outfit I could wear to Skye's funeral. A stranger bumped into me in one of the crowded boutiques we visited.

"Sorry." I jerked away, an ache forming behind my eyes in the bright lights of the store.

I tried to choose something to wear, but there were too many clothes crowding the racks. I couldn't focus on any one thing.

Turning to Melody, I said, "I'm not feeling so good. Can you take me home?"

"Sure, baby girl." She wrapped a thin arm around me and let me lean heavily against her as we all walked back to the car park. "I'll pull something out of my wardrobe for you to borrow instead."

"That would be great. Thanks." I rubbed my forehead with a clammy hand, trying to relieve the ache that was building there.

Although I was glad to have spent the day with Melody and Gretchen, I was well aware that they would be returning to their normal lives soon, and I would be left trying to figure out how to do life without the person who had made it bearable for me.

CHAPTER

Eight

We got home to discover that Mum was back early. I was glad to see that my suffering had given so many of my family members the opportunity to ditch work. Only Dad had continued going into the office. I didn't think his own death would keep him from his beloved engineering job.

"Nova," Mum said with the now-default pitying look that made me want to disappear as quickly as possible. "Skye's mum rang while you were out. They're bringing her home tomorrow, and Mrs Fletcher said you're welcome to go and see her if you want. Her funeral has been set for Friday."

"Okay," I breathed, tears welling up in my eyes. The thought of Skye's body, and casket, and funeral was just... unbearable. "I'm really tired. I'm going to try and sleep for a bit."

"Sure," Mum agreed, turning towards the kitchen. "I'll wake you for dinner."

Somehow, my sisters and I had failed to eat lunch while we were out, but I wasn't hungry anyway. All I wanted now was time alone to think and process everything I had lost.

Upstairs in my bedroom, I climbed into the bed that used to feel so luxurious. Now it felt unbearably cold and empty. Never again would Skye hang out on it with me, chatting about anything and everything.

Pulling my phone out of my pocket, I flicked open my favourite social media account. The photo of Skye and Ty in their togs at the beach on Sunday evening was top of my feed. And it had over 700 comments. With tears rolling down my cheeks, I read through every single comment, some even as they appeared on the screen. After a while, they all started to blur together... *Skye's gone to her home in the sky... I'll miss you so much... Such a perfect couple... Such a tragedy... I can't believe this happened to you of all people... Taken far too young... You'll make such a beautiful angel in heaven...* On and on the messages went, most of them from people who barely knew Skye. But reading them knocked down my wall again and I cried until I was gasping for air.

Losing Skye was unbearable. It felt like when I was first learning to surf on the rough West Coast and the waves had kept crashing over me, shoving me into the gritty sand, stealing my breath, and scouring me raw. Every time I'd sprung up to the surface to try and breathe, another wave had barrelled into me, hurling me into the ground like an enraged giant until I couldn't tell up from down or limb from limb.

Losing Skye felt exactly like that, and I wrung myself raw on my tears. It was only when a lull in the waves finally came that I was able to drift off to sleep.

Mum's hand on my shoulder eventually brought me back to the surface.

"Nova. It's dinner-time," she murmured.

Groggily, I descended the stairs to find my entire family waiting for me in the lounge. Even my eldest sister, Veronica, was there along with her husband, Mark, and their two kids, Arlo and Paton. They must have driven up from Cambridge especially to be here for me.

That meant a lot.

When I was little, I had one hundred per cent believed Veronica was my real mother. She looked the most like me and, because she was the eldest, was the one who took the most care of me while Mum was depressed. I'd developed this whole theory where I was her secret love child, but because she was young and unmarried, nobody wanted me to know the truth so they had just pretended I was Mum's baby. I even thought they had written a clue into my name by giving me a "V" like her.

But then, when I was seven, Veronica moved down to Palmerston North to study veterinary medicine and I was completely devastated. She was 21 by then and had been working for a few years after high school to save for her five-year course of study. I thought she had stayed home for me, so when she left, my whole world turned upside down. I felt so abandoned.

Slowly, I built up my walls against her so that, by the time she came back to Auckland for her mid-semester visit, I was able to pretend she didn't matter to me anymore. After a while, I even came to believe it. Over the past decade, we'd become virtual strangers. Still, it meant a lot to me that she and Mark were here now, when I needed them most.

"Hey, everyone." I curled my fingers in a gentle wave as I did a hasty sweep of the room with my eyes. Hating to be the centre of attention, I quickly focused my gaze on my adorable niece. "Hey, sweetheart." I scooped eight-month-old Paton out of Mark's arms and into a cuddle that was instantly soothing to my grieving soul. Her milky baby smell offered a timeless comfort. "You've grown so much since I last saw you!"

Paton cooed back at me, a delighted smile lighting up her face.

Not wanting to miss out on Aunty Nova time, Arlo wrapped his short arms around one of my legs to get my attention. I passed Paton back to Mark and picked up Arlo instead. "How's my favourite boy in the whole world?" I asked him.

"Dat Batman," he confidently announced, holding up a *Duplo* Batman figurine in his dimpled fist.

"Ooooh, that is Batman," I replied. "Very cool. Almost as cool as you are!"

Everyone kept standing around watching me awkwardly until Mum told us to head through to the dining room. I carried Arlo in and took a seat at our long table, settling him onto my lap. Veronica sat down beside me and pulled Paton's high chair up to the table on her other side.

Mum had cooked us a feast fit for the holidays. A lesser table would have been straining under the weight of slow-cooked lamb and gravy, roast kumara and pumpkin, three kinds of salads, minted peas, broccoli, and cheese sauce. Under normal circumstances this would have been so special. Tonight, though, it felt like we were acting out the stage play of a family dinner – everyone being careful to say their lines and play their part.

Dad said grace from his seat at Mum's left, thanking God that he'd married such a fine cook. We chuckled, which was the reaction he was hoping for, and then he asked God to comfort us as we mourned the loss of Skye. The mood shifted, and we all said, "Amen," right on cue.

After grace, Veronica quickly put together a Peter Rabbit bowl loaded up with peas, smashed roast vegetables, and lamb diced into tiny pieces for Arlo, then passed it to me.

"Yum," I whispered into Arlo's fluffy blonde head. "Look at all this good *kai*, Arlo."

He was too busy picking up pieces of lamb and shoving them into his mouth to answer me.

"Don't let him keep shovelling that lamb in," Veronica warned me as she fed Paton, "or he'll be chewing all night."

"One piece at a time, Arlo," I said, stilling his hand before he could pop another piece of lamb into his overstuffed mouth.

Then Veronica turned from Paton to place a gentle hand on

my forearm and say, "I'm really sorry about Skye. I know how close you were."

"Thank you," I said. And, even though I couldn't say it to her face, I was *really* glad Veronica was there.

CHAPTER

Nine

I got back from an early run on Wednesday morning to discover a text from Ty: *Mum's driving me to Skye's at 10. Would you like a ride?*

I smiled at his perfect text message punctuation and also at the knowledge that I wouldn't have to go and see Skye alone. Ty was my safety – the person who grounded me and comforted me like no one else could. I was grateful that we were going through this nightmare together. I texted him back: *I'd appreciate that. Thank you.*

Ty: *No thanks necessary. This will be easier with you at my side.*

Nova: *Right back at ya.*

Skye was the first thing I saw when Ty and I walked into the Fletchers' lounge. She was laid out in a polished coffin right in the middle of the floor, and there's something about a dead body that's hard to ignore. I hadn't expected her to be *right* there. I'd figured she'd be off in a side room somewhere, and I'd have time to prepare for the sight of her, but there was no time. Ty flinched beside me like he too had been caught off guard, so I decided to be brave for both of us and approach her coffin straight away.

Mrs Fletcher intercepted me with a hug. "I'm glad you could

come," she said. Her brown eyes were so swollen with tears, she was barely recognisable as Skye's mother.

"Thank you for inviting me," I replied, squeezing her. "I actually came to the hospital too, but they wouldn't let me see her. I didn't know if I'd ever see her again."

"Oh! Sweetheart." Mrs Fletcher sniffed back tears, and I rubbed her back in slow circles to comfort her.

She eventually released me and turned to give Ty a hug too. "How are you holding up, dear one?" she asked him.

"I've had better days," he mumbled over her shoulder, his eyes drifting to Skye's coffin again. His complexion was turning a worrying shade of grey as he took in the sight of Skye's motionless body. "How are you doing with everything?"

"Oh, you know. Terribly." Mrs Fletcher shrugged, stepping back out of his embrace and lifting a hand to gently touch the bandage on his chin. "I still can't believe any of this is real – that Skye's really gone."

"I know." Ty shook his head. "And I'm so unbelievably sorry about the accident. It's killing me. I hope you know that."

"I do know that, Ty, and I forgive you," she said. "I don't want you holding onto guilt. Do you think you could let go of it, for my sake? It would just add to my burden if I knew you were beating yourself up over what happened."

"I'll try." Ty pressed his lips together, overcome by her grace.

Mrs Fletcher patted his cheek softly and then nodded for us to go and see Skye. I smiled sadly at her and stepped towards the casket that contained my closest friend in the world. Skye looked like a wax model of herself. Almost identical to the original, but with the most vital part of her missing; her soul was no longer in residence.

Ty worked his bottom lip in and out of his mouth as he stared down at his dead girlfriend. His grief was apparent in his own waxen appearance and the tiny shudders that rippled through his body. I tentatively lifted a hand to his back, and he sagged into me. Together, we sank to our knees on the thick carpet beside Skye's coffin.

Neither of us said anything. We just clung to each other as we gazed at her body lying there so utterly still. Someone had pulled an ivory silk sheet over Skye's chest, and I wondered what sort of damage it was hiding. The funeral people had plastered her face with thick foundation and unnatural amounts of blusher, I guess to give her colour. They'd also styled her golden hair around her head in loose waves, and it looked perfect – her curls finally behaving like they never had in life.

It was weird because I knew she wasn't really there, but I kept expecting her to wake up and talk to me anyway. A couple of times I even thought I saw her twitch, but I had to remind myself it was just my eyes playing tricks on me.

As I stared at her, my eyes kept drifting to the bump on her nose where she'd broken it playing rugby. I wanted to smooth it out for her because that bump had always bothered her, especially set above her pointy chin like it was. She'd often complained that the combination of nose and chin made her look a bit too rodent-like, but I'd only ever thought they made her face more interesting. She'd dyed her hair blonde as a way of distracting people's attention from the facial details she didn't adore about herself, and it had worked. Only those closest to her ever realised her nose wasn't completely straight, or that her chin was pointier than some airbrushed ideal – and the people closest to her thought she was beautiful exactly as she was. This was the last time I would ever see that precious, beautiful bump.

"Hey, Skye," I croaked out, and Ty's twitch told me he was surprised by my sudden outburst. "I don't know how I'm supposed to do this," I ploughed on. "How I'm supposed to say goodbye to you and carry on living without my best friend by my side. You've been such an amazing friend to me. I'm going to miss you so much. I already do. I wish you could come back. It doesn't seem fair that you're going to miss out on the whole rest of your life. You always lived life bigger and better than the rest of us. I'm really going to miss that about you. I miss you so much. Did I say that already? It's all I can think about – how much I miss you and how that feeling is *never* going to go away. I don't know what to do. I wish you could tell me what to do. I feel hollowed out now, you know? Like that awful movie we watched where the cloned people had to give up their internal organs so the original people could stay healthy. I'm one of those gutted clones now, trying to survive with only one lung and a piece of a liver."

Ty snort-laughed beside me.

I nudged his shoulder and then reached out a hand to touch Skye's cheek, thinking it would feel like it always had – warm and soft – but it was hard and cold, like chilled clay, and it shocked me so much, I yanked my hand back and tucked it into my hoodie pocket.

Ty must have taken courage from my words though, because he began speaking too. "Thank you for being the best girlfriend I could've ever wished for. I'm so sorry for crashing the car. I wish it had been me who'd died, not you. This shouldn't have happened to you. I hope that whenever we meet again, you'll be able to forgive me." He reached out a hand to touch one of her soft curls, but stopped himself before connecting and pulled his hand back into his side, like I had.

I don't think either of us knew what we were supposed to do next. We'd seen Skye and said our last words to her, but once we left, we would never be able to see her again. In the end, we just stayed there for hour after hour, absorbing all the details of her face and keeping vigil over her body.

Behind us, people came and went from the Fletchers' house with gifts of flowers and food, sometimes appearing by our side to view Skye's body, but I was barely aware of them. I had floated away from the physical plane entirely. When Rosamie Tyler placed her hand on my shoulder to tell me it was time to go, it was a lead weight dragging me back down to earth with a heavy thud.

CHAPTER

Ten

Having been to all of my grandparents' funerals over the years, I thought I knew what I was in for. But Skye's Friday morning service was, without a doubt, the most heartbreaking funeral of them all. Whereas my grandparents had lived their whole lives, had families, and done all the things they'd wanted to do in their time on earth, Skye's life had barely started. Her death was such a senseless waste, and that was reflected by the multitude of mourners packing our church inside and out.

Laingholm High School had closed for the morning so that staff and students could attend the funeral, but they mostly congregated in the parking lot and side hall rather than inside the main church. Screens and speakers had been set up so they could still watch the service.

Wearing a simple charcoal dress of Melody's, I took a seat in one of the reserved rows near the front of the church. Mr and Mrs Fletcher had asked me to give a eulogy. Ty had also been asked to speak, and he was sitting on the end of the row in front of me, next to his parents and older sister, Alex, who had flown up from *Otago University* to be with Ty while he grieved.

After Pastor Bailor said a brief beautiful message about Skye's brief beautiful life, he called me to the stage. I clutched a piece of refill paper in my hand and stepped up to the wooden podium, feeling like it would have been so much easier to speak in front of the crowd with Skye standing next to me. She'd always given me courage to do the impossible. That ridiculous thought had me hitching my breath, and for a few seconds I teetered on the edge of tears, but I managed to pull myself back with a loud throat clear before launching into my prepared eulogy.

"There was something about Skye that always challenged me to *live* bigger, try harder, and dare more. She had this cocky way of looking at me that egged me on in the best possible way. The first time I talked to her, we were eight and Skye had just started at *Laingholm Primary*. I think it might have been her very first lunch there when she strode up to me, thrust a hand on her hip, and said, "Well? Are you going to play rugby with me or not?" I looked behind me, wondering who she was talking to because it obviously wasn't me – the tallest, skinniest, shyest girl in our year. *I'd* never made plans to play rugby with her. But she just kept standing there, waiting for me to agree. It was like she'd sized up all the girls at our school and figured out *I* was the one who'd be most up for getting smashed by the boys on the rugby field. And she was right. I just hadn't known it until she'd pointed it out to me.

"From that moment on, we were inseparable. I've been so, *so* lucky to call Skye my best friend for almost ten years. I wish it had been longer. Like, forever. But I'm grateful for the years I did get and know how utterly blessed I've been. Over the past decade, Skye has adventured with me through school and church, on the rugby field, in the surf, and everywhere else that either of us dared the other to go. She's also brought ridiculous amounts of humour and silliness to my life. More than that though, she's lived her life with integrity and a strong faith in God that has encouraged me in my own faith. I'm a better person for having known her and I'm going to miss her more than I think even *I* know."

Turning towards Skye's coffin, which was closed and adorned

with a wreath of pink peonies she would have loved, I did start to cry as I said, "Goodbye my darling friend. You ran the good race and I have no doubt you were hollered through the gates of heaven. I'm looking forward to meeting you there one day. Until then, go with all my love."

I blew her a kiss, then wiped my tears with the back of my hand as I stepped down from the stage and teetered back to my seat. My three sisters all tried to embrace me simultaneously.

As they petted me, Pastor Bailor stepped back up to the pulpit and said, "Thank you for those beautiful words, Nova. I've been privileged to witness your friendship with Skye develop over the years, from Sunday School to Youth Group, and I know you were a blessing to her just as much as she was a blessing to you."

Turning to face the rest of the mourners in the hall, Pastor Bailor then said, "And now I would like to ask Skye's boyfriend, Andrew Tyler, to take the stage."

Ty stood up and turned around to pull out a guitar from under his seat. Everyone sat up straighter in their seats. Ty cut such a handsomely tragic figure in his black suit. It looked extra crisp in comparison to his messy hair, which he'd obviously been pushing back from his forehead all morning.

Catching my gaze, he flashed me a nervous wish-me-luck smile before straightening his shoulders and turning to march up to the low stage, guitar in hand. Reaching the pulpit, Ty took a few seconds to collect himself, plug in his guitar, and tune it before leaning into the microphone and saying, "*Magandang umaga*. Good morning. I'm Ty. This is a song I wrote for Skye, for today. She was always asking me to write her something, and I'm really wishing I'd done it when she was still here to appreciate it."

He dropped his head to focus on his guitar as he began picking the strings in a simple repeating melody. Then he took a deep breath, looked up towards the windows at the back of the church and sang:

At seventeen, you've barely seen
Anything, of anything.
A girl like you, faithful and true
Deserved to see her whole life through.

An audible gasp sounded around the church and I'm pretty sure everyone *immediately* began to cry.

You should've had ten thousand more
Memories, to bring to shore.
A wedding dress,
A wedding night,
A golden child,
With hair so wild.
A girl like you, faithful and true
Deserved to see her whole life through.

Ty sang with his eyes closed, his head tilted back. I watched the veins in his bronzed neck strain as he broke over the song. His usual rich and melodious voice cracked several times. He was barely holding it together, but it only made the song more beautiful.

I know you're in a better place,
where you've been met by holy grace.
I'm choosing not to fear for you.
I'm choosing now to let you go,
Even as I wonder why
The sun would shine without its Skye.

You should've had ten thousand more
Memories, to bring to shore.

A wedding dress,
A wedding night,
A golden child,
With hair so wild.
A girl like you, faithful and true
Deserved to see her whole life through.

'Cause seventeen, ain't anything
Compared to what, it might've been.
A girl like you
Faithful and true
Deserved to see
Her whole life through.

He finished the song with a final strum and then hung his head, breathing raggedly. The church watched him in stunned silence. His loss was so plain and painful.

Like mine. Like all of ours.

Normally, a song like that would've had those terribly familiar waves knocking me off my board and shoving me underwater, but not this time. No, something had struck me as I had watched Ty sing and been struck breathless once again by my feelings for him. Skye was gone, so there was technically no reason why I couldn't be with Ty if he ever wanted me like I wanted him.

Of course, the second I thought that, I was so ashamed that I wanted to remove my brain from my skull. I mean, seriously! What kind of person would even think about that at her best friend's funeral? A narcissistic monster, that's what kind. I refused to be *that* person. Skye deserved so much better from me.

But how was I supposed to stay friends with Ty now that there was technically nothing getting in the way of a relationship with him? Because I knew myself, and no matter how much self-control I normally had, the pull towards Ty already felt way bigger than me.

Without Skye offering a counter-pull, Ty was my new centre of gravity.

CHAPTER

Eleven

Skye's funeral service concluded with the Chris Tomlin worship song, *Good Good Father*, and if it hadn't been for the Communion that I'd taken with Ty earlier in the week, I think it would have been impossible to sing the words. I was trying to trust that God was a good father, even if it felt like he had just stood by and watched while my best friend died, ignoring my prayers and everyone else's.

In my head, I knew the reality was so much richer than that. Skye's death would have ended in even worse tragedy if Jesus hadn't stepped in and taken her sin upon his own shoulders, granting her eternity and reconciliation with God. But I missed my friend and if God had intervened, I wouldn't have to, so my heart didn't know what to do with that.

When the song finished, six pallbearers stepped forward to carry Skye's coffin out of the church. Ty was one of them. He grabbed the front left handle of the coffin, and I couldn't even imagine how agonising it must've been for him, holding Skye for the last time in *that* way. Skye's dad grabbed the front right handle so he could walk Skye down the aisle in a nightmare version of the wedding day walk he had undoubtedly looked forward to taking with her one day. Skye's brother, her uncle, and her oldest male cousin also took up positions around the coffin, and then our pastor stepped down from the stage to grab the last handle. He was more than just the minister presiding over the funeral; he had been Skye's pastor for almost a decade – the man who had baptised her and led her in her faith from child to almost-adult.

The pallbearers hoisted Skye's coffin onto their shoulders and began the slow march down the aisle to Skye's favourite worship song, *Oceans*. It was the song she had been baptised to when she was thirteen because she wanted to trust God to lead her wherever he needed her to go. I choke-cried when we reached the line about trusting without borders, thinking of my dearest friend who had crossed a border beyond my reach.

And then I stepped into the aisle and trailed behind the Fletcher and Tyler families, who trailed after Skye's coffin while clinging to each other for support. My sisters had gathered behind me in a sweet-smelling cloud. Mum and Dad clutched their hands together behind them, but I didn't hold onto anyone as I followed Skye's coffin out to the hearse. With my best friend gone and my relationship with Ty now teetering into dangerous territory, it was time I got used to doing things alone.

Outside, it was eerily silent. I almost expected tumbleweed to roll past. But then that silence was shattered by a haunting call from the carpark. I peered over the short heads of the Fletcher family to see who had called out. A Māori boy from my school repeated the call, and then hundreds of male students standing behind him responded with shouts of their own. As one, the entire group began chanting in Māori, delivering a chilling farewell haka for Skye. Their fierce chants and actions sent shivers down my spine.

The haka transformed those school boys of various sizes and physiques into full-grown warriors. Their muscles flexed as they slapped their thighs and stamped their feet, yelling in unison and looking like nobody you'd ever want to meet in the bush at night.

Skye's pallbearers stood unmoving with her coffin on their shoulders until the very last hiss of the haka was delivered. Only then did they slide her into the hearse.

In the awed silence that followed, Pastor Bailor held up a basket of peonies and said, "As we say our final goodbyes to Skye, the Fletcher family has requested that anyone who would like to place a flower on Skye's coffin in memory, does so now."

He placed the basket of peonies next to Skye's coffin in the hearse, and people immediately began filing up to take a flower and pay their last respects.

Skye was being cremated after the service, and only her immediate family was invited to attend, so this moment really was goodbye for most of us. I wouldn't have wanted to go to her cremation anyway. The thought of my wild, water-loving Skye burning away was... just.... *No.*

I chose the most beautiful peony I could find in the basket, one that had barely started to unfurl its dozens of petals, and then I kissed it and reached forward to place it at the head of the coffin. "I won't ever forget you," I promised Skye, before stepping back from the hearse and my best friend forever.

"Hey, Nova," a male voice said from behind me.

I turned to find Matthias Smith and Peter Liu watching me uncertainly.

"Hey, dudes." I sad-smiled. "I didn't see you in the service."

"Nah, we waited outside with the school crew so we could do the haka," Matthias explained. "We wanted to vent our rage."

"I respect that." I nodded. "The haka was awesome. You guys gave me literal chills."

"Cool." Peter grinned and then shook his head like he'd just remembered where we were. "How are you holding up?"

"I've had better days." I shrugged. What else was there to say? How did I make funeral small talk when my life was in tatters?

"You spoke well." Peter lifted his eyebrows encouragingly.

"We were watching on the screen. I couldn't believe you held it together."

"Uh, thanks," I said. Maybe I was supposed to be crying more than I was. I didn't know how to do any of this right.

"We heard Ty's song too," Matthias piped in. "Liu here was begging for a hankie after the first line."

I chuckled, which surprised me. But then Peter's eyes shifted to someone walking up behind me, and the upward tilt of his gaze told me exactly who he was looking at. My tallest friend / secret love, Andrew Tyler, was incoming.

The thing was, I so badly wanted to talk to him. Not only was he the one person who understood what I was going through, but I was that one person for him. I wanted to be there for him, but I had no idea how to act normally around him anymore. I could *feel* his approach, and it had birds flapping erratic beats in my chest.

Before Ty could reach us, I bid a hasty farewell to Peter and Matthias.

"I'm going to give my condolences to the Fletchers," I told the boys, rushing off without looking Ty's way.

And then, with the powers that my unburied love for Ty had apparently granted me, I continued to feel his eyes on my retreating back the entire time I walked across the courtyard. Several times over the following hour, I felt his gaze brush against my face, begging me to look his way. It took all of my self-control not to respond.

He needed friends around him who could be just that – friends.

I was no longer that person for him and didn't think I ever could be again.

CHAPTER

Twelve

Mum gave me the afternoon after the funeral off school but said, "I expect you to head back in on Monday."

We were in the final term of the school year and I had assessments in every subject I needed to complete before I could move up to Year 13. I probably could have applied for Compassionate Consideration and moved up anyway, but some stubborn part of me wanted to earn it.

Moping around home wasn't helping me in any case. On Saturday, I went for my usual morning run and then another afternoon one because running was the only thing I could do that made me feel like I had any control over my life.

As I gulped down water after my second brutal run of the day, my phone started ringing on the kitchen bench beside me. The name that flashed on the screen was *Skye Fletcher*, accompanied by a laughing photo of her.

What the heck? I jumped back, frightened. Was someone playing a sick joke on me?

In trepidation, I picked up my phone and tapped to answer. "Hello," I whispered uncertainly.

"Hi, Nova," a woman's voice spoke down the line.

"Who is this?" I asked warily.

"It's Gloria Fletcher," Skye's mum said in a tone of voice that made it clear that should have been obvious.

"Oh! Mrs Fletcher! You just gave me the biggest fright. You realise you've rung me from Skye's phone? It was her name that came up on my screen just now."

Mrs Fletcher gasped when she realised what she had done. "I'm so sorry, Nova. I didn't even think about that. I just wanted to get hold of you and knew that your number would be on Skye's phone. I'm truly sorry."

"That's okay," I reassured her. "My heartbeat's starting to return to normal now. What was it you were ringing about?"

"Well, I've spent the day going through Skye's things, trying to work out what to do with them. I wondered if you'd like to come and take some mementos to help you remember her."

"Oh wow! That's a really kind offer, Mrs Fletcher. Thank you. I'd love that."

"You're welcome, sweetheart. There is one other thing."

"Yeah?" I asked, feeling more than a little wary again.

"I found Skye's diary in her side table and am desperate to read it, but I wondered whether I could give it to you first to vet for me. You knew Skye so well. You could check the diary over to see if it contains anything you think Skye wouldn't have wanted her parents to know about her. Would you be willing to do that?"

"Of course!" I exclaimed. Now I was dying to read the diary too. It would be like hearing Skye's own thoughts again. The next best thing to talking to her. "What if I come around this evening to look through Skye's things and pick up the diary?"

"That would be perfect. I really appreciate it, Nova. Thank you."

"No worries. I'll see you in a couple of hours. I'd come now, but I need to wait until Mum gets home from the supermarket, so I can borrow her car."

"All right then, dear one. I'll see you when you get here."

It was a long wait until Mum got home, now that I had something to look forward to. I pounced on her as soon as she walked in the door, and she lifted a startled hand to her heart. "Nova! You scared me," she gasped. "You can't do things like that. I'm not as young as I look."

"Sorry, Mum. But can I please borrow your car to go to Skye's house? Mrs Fletcher wants me to look through Skye's things and pick out some mementos."

"Okay, sweetheart." Mum smiled sympathetically at me. "But I think I'll drive you. I'd like to give my condolences to Gloria in person and check how she's doing. Help me unload the groceries and then we'll go."

At Skye's house, Mum and Mrs Fletcher sat down together for a cup of tea. Mrs Fletcher told me the diary was on Skye's bedside table and that I was welcome to take anything else from her room I wanted. "No sense in just letting it sit there gathering dust," she explained with a stoic expression. "And I already went through everything this morning and took out all the things of hers I want to keep, so don't worry about stepping on any toes."

With that reassurance, I darted down the hallway to Skye's peach and gold wall-papered bedroom. It was tidier than I'd ever seen it. No dirty clothes slung over chairs. No school books scattered on her desk. Everything was ordered and in its place, and I crumpled in on myself when I saw it. The life had gone out of Skye's bedroom, just like it had gone out of her body. Sinking to the floor, I leaned against the wall next to her door, trying to take a full breath as I absorbed her lifeless room.

My tears came slowly this time, tiredly. But they still ached as much as my sobs had. All of me ached these days. I was growing weary of it, but there was nothing I could do but live through it. Pain demands to be felt.

When my tears had trailed off enough that I could see clearly, I pushed myself back to my feet and walked across the room to where Skye's diary was lying on her bedside table. On its cover was a picture of a sunset-lit beach, which was so typically Skye, it made me smile. I picked it up and held it to my chest for a moment, relishing the opportunity in front of me. Inside of this book were her words. Her inner-most thoughts. What a precious gift that was, now that I could no longer talk to her.

Lying down on the tie-dyed peach and white duvet that covered Skye's bed, I was immediately enveloped by her scent – a mixture of hair product and moisturiser I knew better than anyone's. It brought me comfort and pain in equal measures, but I decided to embrace the comfort as I opened her diary to the first page.

28 September

Dear Diary,

I've never had a diary before, but I'm bestowing this honour upon you because, from the first moment I saw your ~~cover~~ face, I knew you were a kindred spirit. I know we'll be good friends by the end of this. Feel the honour.

You're probably curious about why I've started my first diary at the ripe old age of 16, so here it is: I think that all of my dreams might finally be about to come true. Ty (AKA Andrew Tyler. AKA the most beautiful, amazing, kind, fun, hot boy in the universe) has started looking at me differently. I can't really describe it, but there's an interest behind his heavenly brown eyes that didn't used to be there.

I mean, I've loved him since the day I met him and always thought we'd get together eventually, but, to be honest, I was starting to give up hope. I thought I'd been permanently friend-zoned, and it was killing me.

Don't get me wrong, I'd rather be his friend than nothing. He's an awesome friend. But I LOVE him, Diary. I pine for him. My love would fill an M&M bucket with only red M&Ms, it's that powerful. Understand?

Poor Nova (AKA my best friend, AKA the loveliest person ever) has been hearing me pine over Ty since we were eight years old, and I didn't want to keep inflicting that torture upon her. That's where you come in. I mean, how many times can I expect her to listen to me rave about Ty's perfect bone structure? (For the record: his cheekbones could slice a feijoa like it was butter and his jawline could crack a boulder clean in two.) Nova doesn't understand my obsession. Ty's just Ty to her. How can she not SEE what's living right across the street from her? It boggles the mind, Diary. It really does.

Oh! Diary, I'm so sorry. I just realised that you being my diary is not the honour I so recently built it up to be. You're going to get bombarded with ALL OF MY TY FEELINGS and you won't have any way to run away. Your skinny white pages are so terribly frail.

Deepest apologies. I hope we'll still be friends by the end of this.

Yours affectionately,

Skye Fletcher

Skye's first diary entry from a year ago made me laugh so much, I had to run to the bathroom and empty my bladder. I washed my hands quickly, desperate to get back to her bedroom and read another entry, but Mrs Fletcher spotted me emerging from the bathroom and asked if I'd picked out what I wanted to take home with me. The look on her face told me she was ready for us to leave. Maybe the sight of me in the hallway had been too familiar, too much a reminder of what she had lost.

I shook my head and told her I would get onto picking out what I wanted to keep, but that meant I had to ignore the diary while I looked around Skye's room for things I would miss if I never saw them again. I chose a few clothes from her wardrobe that might fit over my taller frame and then ran my finger along her bookshelf, looking for the books she'd loved that I didn't own – mostly biographies of elite sportspeople. Reading them might help me to feel closer to her again, like reading her diary was doing.

After making my selection, I grabbed the framed photo of us she had on her chest of drawers and laid it flat on top of my newly acquired pile of books. I left behind the framed photo of her and Ty that was also on the dresser, figuring Mrs Fletcher would offer that to him. Adding Skye's diary to the pile of things I'd chosen, I exited her bedroom with one last look over my shoulder at the place I'd spent so much time in before, and never would again.

There was no turning back time. Life kept marching forward, widening the gap between my life with Skye and my life without her.

CHAPTER

Thirteen

The rest of my Saturday night was devoted to Skye's diary. I binge-read it so hard when I got home, I started thinking of *Diary* as a real person with real feelings painfully overshadowed by Skye's love for Ty.

The most exciting entry was the one she'd written the day after my 16th birthday party.

5 October

Dear Diary,

I'm not even going to waste your time trying to make you guess what happened last night. I'm just going to tell you. See how kind I am to you? It's because I'm in the best mood of my WHOLE life.

The most wonderful thing has finally happened to me, and I feel like absolutely anything is possible right now. Like, I could find a unicorn in the enchanted forest behind school and befriend it and learn all of its secrets. Or, I could dance all night in my highest heels, you know the ones that make my feet arch like I'm a super flexible foot model? And I WOULDN'T EVEN GET SORE FEET. That's how perfect everything feels right now.

So, I know I told you I wasn't going to make you guess my good news, but after that long introduction, I'm pretty sure you've already guessed it anyway...

Ty asked me out last night. Squeeeeeeeeeeeeeeeee! (And I said yes, obv.)

I'm so happy, I could scream.

Here's how it happened...

We all went out to dinner for Nova's sweet 16th at the most romantic little Italian restaurant in town, and I dressed up in my hottest dress – you know, the purple one with the plunging backline? I looked good. I felt good. And Ty didn't take his eyes off me all night.

He was looking like the lad he is in a white shirt and fitted navy dress pants. His mum always makes him dress up for Nova's birthday parties. It's so sweet (and hot). Peter and Matthias looked like complete slobs next to him in their saggy jeans and jumpers. Guys really shouldn't underestimate the power of a crisp shirt. Diary, if you're a guy (and I always kind of imagine you are), remember that li'l titbit.

So anyway, we ate our dinner (I had the fettuccine. It was delicious, thanks for asking), and Ty watched me the whole time. I don't think I stopped blushing once. I kept fanning my face and saying, "My, isn't it hot in here?" like I was a Southern Belle or something.

After Mattie had finished eating our mains for us, the guys voted we wander up the street to the cafe with the board games (because they're all nerds) (even Ty a little bit, but he makes up for it in other ways). I convinced them to go dancing instead. I don't think Pete and Mattie would have gone for it except I spoke telepathically to Nova, and she told them that's what she wanted to do for her birthday. God bless her beautiful soul.

It was a dream night. We went to that little underage club on K Road with the fairy lights (you know, the one that's super cute and not at all dodgy) and we danced in a circle for ages until Mattie complained it was making his beer belly jiggle too much. He and Peter went to sit down. Then I spoke telepathically to Nova again, and she went and sat down too.

Suddenly it was just me and Ty on the dance floor.

He took my right hand in his.

And placed his left hand on my hip.

And pulled me towards him.

So, I put my left hand on his shoulder.

And nestled into him.

And we slow-danced.

To Twenty-One Pilots.

It was beautiful.

After the song finished, Ty leaned into my ear and shout-whispered (because the next song had already started and it was really loud), "Do you want to go out with me?"

I just grinned at him and nodded.

And then, Dear Diary, I stretched up on my tippiest of tip toes (because Ty is ridiculously tall and I'm a shortie)

and ...

I KISSED HIM.

And then I fainted. No, not really. But, holy stars, I could have. I love him that much.

The End and Goodnight.

From your best (and only) friend,

Skye Fletcher

I cried for a long time after reading that entry. Skye had finally got everything she'd ever wanted. She'd been completely happy and in love with Ty, and it had all been ripped away from her. Not only that, but her supposed best friend in the whole world was pining after the guy she'd so desperately loved.

My insides were an over-played pinball machine. The course in front of me was clear. I had to stay away from Ty no matter what.

I loved Skye, and she deserved all the honour and respect I could give her. Nine years of friendship deserved that, at the very least.

CHAPTER

Fourteen

The trouble with going back to school was that I normally caught the bus with Ty, and… now I was avoiding him.

I managed to get out of Monday's bus ride by dragging my feet so much after my morning run that I missed the bus completely. Mum gave me a ride to school but told me "in no uncertain terms" that I needed to get myself sorted for Tuesday. Where was *her* compassionate consideration?

Luckily, I didn't have any classes with Ty, so that made avoiding him during the day on Monday fairly easy. Pre-Skye's death, I used to eat lunch with our group on the tiered seating overlooking the school field, but now that Skye was gone, and I couldn't convince my heart to not be shamelessly in love with her one true love, I decided to go to the library instead.

Problem solved.

On Tuesday morning, I crept down to the end of my street, peeking around the corner towards the bus stop across the road. Ty was already there, looking at his phone. I pulled my head back in behind a hedge and watched for the bus to approach. Only when it had driven past, its brakes had squealed, and its doors had whooshed open did I run across the road towards the bus and jump on, sliding through the doors just before they closed and the bus pulled away from the curb. Ty had already walked to our usual seat at the back beside Peter and Matthias, but the bus was now in motion so I scanned my bus card and swung into the seat behind the driver. I leaned my head against the window, aiming for inconspicuousness.

When we got to school, I was the first person off the bus, so I was able to rush to my homeroom without saying anything to the guys.

That tactic worked so well, I used it for Wednesday, Thursday, and Friday too. I managed to get through the whole school week without making eye contact with Ty or talking to him at all. I did catch him looking at me a couple of times with a hurt and puzzled expression on his face. That definitely sucked, I had to admit.

Ignoring his text messages was even worse. But if he knew about my totally inappropriate feelings for him and the way they'd risen so selfishly to the surface at his girlfriend's funeral, he'd be looking at me with horror on his face, so this was a lot more preferable to that. Besides, I doubted he missed me that much, especially since he still had Peter and Matthias to keep him company. I was the one who had been left with nobody. But it was for the best – me keeping my distance from him. I didn't trust myself where he was concerned. I cared about him too much.

All this subterfuge meant that school became something I endured while I waited to go home, where I cuddled my cat or studied for exams while I waited to sleep, where I passed an oblivious few hours before I could run again. And running was what I did to breathe and forget that I was missing the two most crucial people in my life.

Actually, the three most crucial people. I had also stopped talking to God, and I couldn't bring myself to go back to church after the funeral. Skye wasn't there to hang out with anymore, and my grief over her had morphed into bitterness towards God.

I had always suspected he didn't love me that much – that he was disappointed in me somehow – but when he took away my only female friend, it really cemented it for me.

Since God could see right into the heart of me, he must have been able to see that I wasn't worth much. No point answering *my* prayers, when I'd asked him to save Skye. No sir, answered prayers were for the worthy, and that clearly wasn't me.

I checked out of everything and wasn't surprised that my parents failed to notice or care. When had they ever?

CHAPTER

Fifteen

Grief for Skye weighed me down in almost all of my waking moments, and in many of my sleeping ones too.

To have had a best friend – someone to share my thoughts and feelings with, someone who *got* me and genuinely liked me – and then to have lost that friendship in such a sudden and permanent way was unbearable. And even though she hadn't known about my feelings for Ty, that was the only secret I had ever kept from her. Skye had known everything else there was to know about me. Now, all of that knowledge had vanished with her.

It was me and only me against the world.

I tried so hard not to think about Skye when I was at school because the second she even crossed my mind, tears immediately followed. There were certain places where I would normally have seen her or met up with her after different classes, but where her absence was so stark to me now that I had to go out of my way to avoid them. Several times a day I found myself taking the long way around to class, just to avoid the sight of where Skye should have been.

It wasn't enough. As hard as I tried to avoid thinking of her, I still had to visit the bathroom or sick bay several times a week, just to have a place to go. Our school nurse, Mrs Tapere, was so kind to me. If no one else was in the sick bay, she'd set me up on the bed and close the door behind me to give me privacy.

But privacy wasn't the problem. I was constantly alone with my thoughts and pain. I had no one to talk to; no one I trusted enough *to* talk to. Skye had earned my confidence over many, many years. She was irreplaceable to me.

Without a trusted friend to confide in, I tried not to think too much at all. I distracted myself with schoolwork and running, and started going to bed earlier and earlier, just to fill the hours. Sometimes I fell asleep so early, I missed dinner, but I rarely felt hungry any more. My life was one endless nothing.

I was so checked out from life, I don't know how I even noticed it in the low morning light. But, stumbling up our driveway after a pre-dawn run in late-October, I spotted a lone tui sitting in our kōwhai tree. All the flowers had fallen off, so I wasn't sure what it was doing there. I don't think it knew what it was doing there either. Maybe remembering the good old days of friends and flowing nectar. The bird wasn't moving or singing its usual beautiful tui song.

To be honest, it looked kind of miserable.

CHAPTER
Sixteen

One month into my self-imposed exile, Mum knocked on my bedroom door after dinner. I was sitting at my desk, studying for my biology final while I listened to melancholy Harry Styles music. I paused the music and swivelled around in my computer chair to see what Mum wanted.

There was still a bit of light making its way inside through the dormer window above my desk, but Mum switched on the bedroom light anyway as she edged her way into my room.

"How are you doing, sweetie?" she asked me as she sat down on the side of my bed, concern creasing her brow.

"Umm, okay I guess," I replied. It was obviously a lie – I could barely see the point of my life anymore.

Mum scrunched her bottom lip up over her top teeth in disbelief and said, "Well, your father and I are very worried about you. You haven't been yourself since Skye's death. We thought it was best to give you the space you needed to deal with your grief, but… Nova… you're not dealing with it. You've shut everybody out of your life and that's not healthy. Is there more going on here that we don't know about?"

I was actually surprised she had noticed. It seemed like she and Dad had just carried on with life as normal, completely ignoring my distress.

In that moment, a whole lifetime's worth of pain and disappointment with Mum launched itself to the surface, and I couldn't stop myself from asking the question that had always haunted me: "Why don't you love me?"

Mum gasped. Her face drained of colour. I watched it happen. She clenched and unclenched the duvet on either side of her and then asked, "Is that truly what you think? That I don't love you?"

"Of course!" I exclaimed, shocked she would even question something that was so obviously true. "How could I think anything else? You hated being around me when I was little, and you never hug me or tell me you love me. I feel like I'm the unwanted child you've been forced to put up with."

"Oh, Nova!" Mum sounded despairing. "That couldn't be further from the truth. You were my miracle baby and God has used your life to bless me so much. I had no idea you felt this way. You've always seemed so self-contained and sure of yourself."

"Well, it's a lot easier to be self-contained than to put your trust in other people when they're just going to disappoint you."

"Oh, darling," Mum sighed. "That's such a sad way to live. To be sure, nobody's perfect. Everybody's going to let you down sometimes, but we were made for community. It's where all of our joy and growth comes from."

Still angry, I shrugged and repeated my question in a slightly different way: "So, you don't find me difficult to love?"

"Not at all!" Mum leaned forward and fixed her blue eyes on mine. "But I can understand where you would have got that impression, and there's something you need to know. Something I should have told you a long time ago, but didn't because I was trying to protect your innocence."

"What, Mum?" I found myself leaning forward too, with a slightly sick feeling in my stomach, which was nestled right alongside a flicker of hope. "What is it?"

"This isn't easy for me to talk about," she stammered, looking down at her lap, "or even to think about, to tell you the truth, but I hope it will explain why I find it so hard to demonstrate my affection for you." She looked at me again, biting her lip as tears began to glisten in the corners of her eyes. Taking a bracing breath, she said, "I don't have very clear memories of it… I must have been very young when it happened…but I'm fairly certain that one of my uncles messed with me physically in ways he shouldn't have."

Horrified, I asked her, "Which uncle?"

"One you've never met. He actually went to prison when I was a teenager because my cousin had him convicted for doing the same thing to her. He's been out of prison for a long time now, but no one in our family has had anything to do with him since he went in."

"Oh, Mum. That is horrible! Did you go to his trial?" I asked.

"No, I never told my parents what he'd done to me. Actually, I never told anybody about it until after you were born, which is why you were my miracle baby."

"Huh?" I huffed, confused.

"I think I must have suppressed any memories of what happened. I actually forgot all about it, if you can believe that. But subconsciously I spent a lot of effort trying to control every detail of my life so that I wouldn't feel powerless again. I planned out my pregnancies with your sisters perfectly, and was so happy that they arrived exactly on time, two years apart from each other. I thought my life was good, but in reality I didn't trust anyone."

"So, what happened when I was born then?" I asked.

"Well, when I was 42, I stopped getting my period. I thought it must be the start of early menopause, so I didn't give it much thought beyond that. I was six months pregnant with you before I even realised."

"Oh wow!" I exclaimed, trying to imagine what that would

have been like. "That must've been a big shock for you."

"It was. It was a huge shock. I hadn't planned for you. I was working in a job I loved, and the girls were all so much older – Melody was almost ten by then. Plus I only had three months to get my head around the fact you were on your way before you arrived. I had never felt so out of control of anything in my adult life."

It felt weird sitting so formally at my desk while Mum was revealing all of these intimate details about her past, so I stood up and moved over to my bed, where I climbed under the duvet cover and leaned against my headboard. Mum swivelled around on the bed, bringing her knees up gracefully and tilting them over to the side.

"So, what happened when I arrived?" I asked her after we had both resettled.

"Well, your actual birth was very traumatic. You were breech, so the labour took a long time and was incredibly painful. I think the trauma of it triggered something in me to remember what my uncle had done to me all those years ago. After you were born, I sunk into postnatal depression, which quickly turned into full-blown depression, and it was a really dark, really hard time for everyone. As soon as I realised what my uncle had done, I told your dad about it. He was livid. Not with me, of course, but with my uncle. Meanwhile, I felt like I was stuck in a nightmare, reliving those hideous memories in my mind over and over."

"I'm so sorry that happened to you," I consoled her.

"Thank you, sweetie. No one deserves to be treated like that by another human being. But the thing is, remembering it and going through the postnatal depression seemed like such a horrible thing at the time, but it was actually the beginning of healing for me. God was able to use that dark time and turn it into something good. I've come to realise that he didn't want me to keep on living a lie. He wanted to set me free from the shame and betrayal of my past, and the only way I could be free was by acknowledging what had happened and working through it – processing the way my uncle had damaged my trust in others as well as the lies I had come to believe about myself."

"What lies?" I asked her.

"Well, the main one I believed was that I was unworthy of love." Mum smoothed the fabric of her linen trousers down over her calves as she spoke. "When my uncle abused me, it made me feel utterly worthless. And part of me blamed my parents for not protecting me from him. I thought it was because they didn't care enough about me, but, in reality, they didn't know it had happened. I never told them. Still, subconsciously I thought that if they had loved me enough, they would have noticed something was wrong. I became someone who tried to control everything in my life, and I thought that gave me safety. After you were born, it took me a number of years and a lot of counselling to realise that I even believed those lies. God has been so patient and gracious with me. He's taught me that I don't have any control in this life. He's in charge. In fact, Jesus guaranteed us that in this world we will have troubles, but we can take heart because he has overcome the world. Even now, God is working to redeem me and convince me that I am loved, and I'm so grateful to him for that."

"So that's why you don't like to be hugged?" I realised aloud. Mum's strange behaviour over the years was finally starting to make sense. "Because of what your uncle did to you?"

"Yes." Mum nodded. "I still hate prolonged physical touch because it reminds me of the way my uncle trapped me with it. The best way I can describe it is that it makes me feel panicky and claustrophobic. At this point, I'm starting to think I might always respond to touch that way. Then again, God has already redeemed so much in my life, maybe he can redeem this too."

Even though I was saddened by what Mum had shared with me, a part of me also felt lighter. What I had experienced as rejection by her now had an explanation that had nothing to do with me. Mum did want me. There were logical reasons why she didn't hug me, and they weren't because there was something wrong with me, or because she didn't love me. All of my assumptions had been wrong.

"I'm really glad you told me this, Mum," I said. "I'm so sorry you had to go through all of that, but I definitely think it's good that I know. At least now I feel like I understand you better."

"I'm glad, Nova," Mum said. "But now I must ask you to forgive me. My actions have caused you to doubt my love for you, and for that I am truly sorry. I do love you my darling child. So much. Will you forgive me?"

"Of course, Mum!" I said. "Of course, I forgive you."

We didn't hug it out, but Mum did pat my leg before she left my room and that was enough, now that I understood why physical touch was so hard for her.

As I waited for sleep to arrive that night, I hoped that the forgiveness I had given Mum was real and would last. I had been so caught up in the moment and overwhelmed by everything she had shared with me that I had just wanted to make her feel better. But now I wondered if it would be that simple to get over. 17 years of heartache were a lot to undo.

Tentatively I prayed to God for the first time in several weeks, *"Lord God, help me forgive Mum for real. I don't want to feel bitter and resentful towards her, so please show me the way through this. Help me to have grace for her like you have for me. You've forgiven me so much, and I know I need to forgive her too, but it still hurts. I don't want to keep blaming her, but I don't think I can get over it without you. Please help me. In Jesus' name. Amen."*

CHAPTER
Seventeen

I was hyperaware of Ty stretching on the sideline as I strode out onto the rubber racetrack for my 1500 metres final in early December. Ty stood a good few inches taller than the other guys around him – although, to be fair, half of that extra height was probably due to his wild mane of black hair. Meanwhile, our school's racing kit of shorts and singlet was showing off his ridiculously tanned and sculpted body in a way that would have had Skye weeping if she were still here.

I almost smiled at that thought.

Ty had subtly positioned himself to watch my race while he stretched, even if we didn't acknowledge each other anymore. I didn't know how to undo the damage I had done to our friendship, or even if I should since I was still trying to honour Skye's relationship with him, so I pretended I didn't see him as I waited for the Official to start us off.

I had plenty to distract me anyway, what with my parents screaming wildly from the side-lines – Mum especially, in a non-typical display of excitement. My race hadn't even started and she was already yelling, "Run, child! Run!"

Things between us had been so much better these past weeks. We had relaxed more than I ever thought possible around each other. It finally felt like we could be real with each other. However, part of me still mourned for what I had lost out on growing up, and what I would probably never have with her – physical affection. My skin ached to be touched by someone, anyone. It pained me to admit how often I daydreamed about that one beautiful day I had spent with Ty in his bedroom after Skye died... waking up with him nestled into my back... hugging each other as we cried.

No. Now was not the time to get distracted by thoughts of Ty. I had a race to run.

I nodded at my mum to signal I'd heard her and then turned to face forwards, visualising the race before me while I shook out my arms and legs.

My hair was pulled back into a tight ponytail, and I was wearing my school's female racing kit. It was a simple combination of black bike pants and a singlet with my racing number pinned to the front and *Laingholm High School* proudly printed on the back. The outfit hung more loosely on my frame than it used to; I had lost quite a bit of weight since Skye died. Grief will do that.

It was actually a big deal to be representing my school here today, not that any of my classmates knew about it, or even cared (other than Ty, of course.) We would have probably had a bigger audience if Ty wore his racing kit to school sometimes.

The weather had put on a glorious display for the final day of the New Zealand Secondary Schools Track and Field Championships – clear blue skies with only the slightest hint of a breeze. We'd just rolled into summer, so the day was nicely sunny without being too hot.

The 1500 metres race was my last one of the weekend, and I was already worrying about what I was going to do when it was over. School was finished for the year, and my summer holidays loomed bleakly before me.

"On your marks..." the Official called from the sideline,

distracting me from my worries as I eagerly stepped up to the white line and got into my starting position.

Crack! The gun snapped when we were all ready, and I launched myself forward on the springy racetrack, pushing myself to get in front of the other runners so I could take the lead and move into the inside lane. Already I was relishing the stretch and pull of my muscles, the expansion of my lungs. It was ironic that running had become the only time I could actually breathe properly. Grief had made me a mutant in that way, but the upside was that I didn't need to save anything for later in the race. I ran like the answers to all life's problems were waiting for me at the finish line.

If only they were.

I won, of course. I'd been winning all weekend, despite being one of the youngest racers in my division. I doubted the other competitors trained anywhere near as much as I did these days, or on such steep hills. There had been a lot of interviews with questions about what my future racing plans were, but I'd kept my answers deliberately vague because I was still just taking it one day at a time.

After completing the 1500 metres, I was already walking around with my hands resting on top of my head to keep my lungs open when a girl from Bethlehem College crossed the finish line to take second place. The rest of the racers burst over the line in a flurry soon after her and immediately collapsed onto the ground to recover.

When the other racers were up to it, I shook their hands and then saw my parents shuffling over to congratulate me.

"I've decided to rename you *Sky Racer – She Who Dances on Light*." My mum laughed at her culturally insensitive joke as she gingerly patted my arm. "Goodness, you're very sweaty." She promptly wiped her hand on her beige capris. "Pass her the drink, Hugh. *Sky Racer* needs to rehydrate."

I had discovered that Mum loved fussing over me when I raced. The drink was her own special concoction – and by "special" I mean a foul and disgusting mixture of apple cider vinegar, coconut water, cayenne pepper, and other obscure ingredients she had read about on the internet.

"Why can't I just drink chocolate milk like the other girls?" I mock-sighed as I reached for her hideous concoction, secretly relishing the newfound affection.

"Because you're a winner, Nova," Mum nodded primly, "and winners don't do what everybody else does."

I laughed. Mum was letting my recent success go a little too much to her head. The truth was, it had nothing to do with me caring about winning, and everything to do with me caring about nothing else. I'd thrown all of my friendships away, and while my mum and I were definitely on better terms, I still suffered from loneliness most of the time.

"Look! The boys just got called to the track." Dad pointed to the starting line. "Let's grab a seat and watch Ty's race."

"Ah, sure Dad." I grimaced, following him and Mum to a row of seats with a good view of the finish line. Ty was still our neighbour and the son Dad had never had, so there was no way I could duck out of watching his race.

Crack! The starting gun echoed across the stadium, and the senior boys launched into their race, immediately vying for the best positions. Ty held back in second place, letting the frontrunner break the wind for him. Smart.

The guys kept to a relatively slow pace for the first two laps. I guess because they didn't have a crackpot like me in their midst, setting a ridiculous speed.

Going into the third lap, they all looked tired and ready for it to be over. I didn't know how they were even going to make it to the end of the lap, let alone the extra three hundred metres after that, but they must've all realised the finish line was near because suddenly everyone began perking up and jockeying each other for better positions as they turned the corner into the final straight.

My parents, along with most of the stadium, began cheering wildly as the competition heated up. I almost tipped off my seat, I was leaning so far forward.

With two hundred metres to go, Ty veered right and put on a sudden burst of speed, stretching his legs in a long loping run that had him overtaking the frontrunner just metres before the finish line and taking the win. I could have burst with pride.

Safely over the finish line, Ty fell to his knees, hands on the ground as he desperately tried to regain his breath.

"What a race!" Dad slapped his thighs joyously. "I wish I'd videoed that for Rosamie and James."

"Uh, I think the organisers have that covered, Dad." I pointed to the professional cameras stationed in the seats above our heads.

"So they do. Well, let's go and congratulate the boy at least."

"You two go ahead," I said. "I'm busting to use the loo. I'll meet you back here soon. Okay?"

It wasn't technically a lie. I kind of needed to use the toilet after downing Mum's brew. But, more importantly, I needed to get away from Andrew Tyler and my never-dying, thoroughly-inappropriate feelings for him.

CHAPTER
Eighteen

Emerging from the girls' toilets, I came face to face with Ty leaning casually against the cinder block wall.

"Oh!" I took a startled step backwards and then tried to cover my surprise by pointing off to my left and saying, "I think the boys' loos are over that way, if you're lost."

"I'm not lost," he replied grimly. "I was waiting for you."

"Oh," I said again, and then bit my bottom lip nervously. "What for?"

"I want to know why you've been ignoring me." He looked down his straight nose at me, through slit eyes. "I want to know why you haven't spoken to me since Skye's funeral. Is it because you blame me for her death? Because I'm pretty sure it was *you* who told me her death was an accident and no one would blame me for it. Which means this silent treatment on your part is pretty cruel, Nova."

"Oh, man." I rubbed my hands across my eyebrows and then looked up into Ty's scowling toffee-brown eyes. "Is that what you thought? That I blamed you?"

He nodded, still scowling, but I could read hurt behind his expression.

"I'm so sorry you took it that way. I promise you, that thought *never* crossed my mind. I don't blame you for Skye's death. Not even a little bit."

"Well, thank God for that." He sighed and dropped his head back against the cement wall, hitting it with a soft *thunk*. A muscle in his angular jaw popped in and out as he clenched his teeth before lifting his head and skewering me with his stare once more. "So, if you don't blame me for the crash… why the cold treatment? I thought you were the one person I could count on to be there for me through all of this, but you've completely ghosted me."

I stared at my bright green running shoes as I scrambled for a way to answer him, feeling deeply ashamed of the way I'd behaved. I should've realised Ty would read my absence as blame. I was an idiot. But what could I say to him? There was actually nothing I could say to explain my behaviour, besides the truth, and that was the one thing he was never going to hear from me.

I opted for a complete non-answer instead: "Ahhh, you know…. things have been rough lately. I needed time to… deal… with everything."

"Well? Have you had enough time?" He asked, drawing his eyebrows together in a frown that did nothing to mar the ridiculous beauty of his tanned face. "Or do you plan on ignoring me a while longer."

"Hey!" I retorted. "I'm allowed to grieve however I need to, for as long as I need to."

"Of course you are." He nodded, opening his eyes extra wide to emphasise how much he agreed with my statement. "But I didn't expect you to be mean about it."

"You think I'm being mean?" I asked softly, scuffing the toe of my shoe against the ground.

"You don't?" He shook his head, baffled.

Man, this was so messed up. How was I going to talk my way out of this?

"I thought you'd be okay," I finally breathed, a notch above a whisper. "You still had Peter and Matthias. I'm the one who's had no one."

"Yeah, but why?" he asked, frustratedly kicking the heel of his shoe against the wall behind him. "You didn't have to be alone. All three of us would've been there for you if you'd let us."

"I had my reasons, Ty. Ones I can't really discuss with you. But please know my heart was in the right place. I care about you a lot." *Way too much, in fact.*

"What the flip, Nova? What kind of answer is that?" Ty groaned, fisting his dark hair on either side of his head. "I've been going crazy over here. Crazy! Do you get that? I killed my girlfriend, which, by the way, was the absolute worst thing ever, but then somehow I lost my best friend in the bargain. You've become a complete ghost, drifting past, but never seeing or acknowledging me. I feel like I killed you too."

"I'm so sorry, Ty," I whispered. "How can I ever make it up to you?"

He fixed me with bleak, thoughtful eyes and then said, "There is one thing you can do for me. I want you to bring me with you whenever you go running."

CHAPTER

Nineteen

The alarm on my phone had me flinging myself out of bed at 5am on Monday morning. I launched myself at my chalk-painted side table to switch it off. The second I'd swiped my screen into silence, the pain of loss clenched me in its grasp, like it did every morning.

It was still true.

Skye was still gone.

I was still *never* going to see her again.

I fell into my early morning routine to try and distance myself from the pain – sliding into a pair of stretchy black exercise pants, a sports bra and comfy t-shirt, good socks (the kind I could trust to stay up), and a new pair of running shoes.

Even though I didn't have anything urgent to train for now that the secondary school championships were over, I *needed* to run. Besides, it was easier to keep up my fitness than try and get it back before a competition.

Mum had prepared a jar of special brew the night before, and it was waiting for me in the fridge downstairs. I chugged a couple of mouthfuls while I stretched my legs against the kitchen bench. Then I set down the rest for later, making my way through the living room and out the front door… where I found Ty sitting on the top step, waiting for me in a running outfit of his own.

"You were serious!" I exclaimed.

"Indeed," he replied, springing to his feet. "Anytime you run, I run too. That's the deal we made. I need a running partner and think you'd be perfect for the job."

"Well," I said, desperately wondering how I was going to keep my heart hidden from him, "good luck keeping up with me."

"Oh really?" A twinkle flashed in his eyes, which looked tarseal-black in the pre-dawn light. "I seem to remember beating you in every race ever. Like, since you first learned to toddle on your shaky little bow legs."

"Whatever. That's just because you're six months older than me," I protested. Then, even though it pulled at my heart horribly, I said, "Race you to the beach."

He was already on the top step, so he had the head start. And he used it. He didn't bother with the rest of the steps, just leapt over them all panther-like to land on the brick path that ran alongside my driveway under an arbour of cherry trees.

Not to be outdone, I slid down the rounded stair railing and landed nimbly on my feet at the bottom, where I took off at a sprint after Ty.

Without looking back to check if I was following him, Ty turned out of my driveway, ran down the slope to the bottom of our road, and darted across Laingholm Drive. I was right on his heels.

He was fast; faster than I'd expected. The muscles in his legs stretched and contracted as he pounded the narrow pavement in front of me, not giving me a chance to overtake him.

We had done the hard yards, getting up the hill and running its crest, and were about to descend it again to the beach when Ty suddenly threw himself onto the bench of a wooden bus shelter. I pulled up short and gaped at him. He was *gasping* for breath.

"Are you okay?" I asked cautiously.

"Just give me a minute," he breathed raggedly.

So, I did. I used the break to stretch against the brown clapboard wall of the bus shelter, trying to keep limber while I waited for Ty to regain his breath.

"That was mental." Ty finally stood up and joined me, stretching against the bus shelter wall. "You're such a sweat. We just sprinted uphill for twenty minutes flat, and you're not even winded. How's that even possible?"

"Oh, it definitely put a strain on my breathing." I shrugged, "But it's the good type of strain, you know? From doing something active. It's a thousand times better than the other kind."

"What other kind?" He drew his eyebrows together.

"Uh..." How to say this without making him feel guilty? "You know, the passive kind that comes from not being able to do anything to save my best friend."

"Oh." He looked away from me, through the trees that were currently blocking our view of the sea. After a strained couple of minutes, in which I just watched his shoulders rise and fall under his grey tee-shirt, he finally said, "Yeah, I know all about that kind of strain." And then he took off running at a breakneck speed down the narrow winding footpath. "Try to keep up," he called over his shoulder before disappearing around the corner.

CHAPTER

Twenty

"I'm back," I called to Mum and Dad as I came through the front door after parting ways with Ty on the road between our two houses. I was strangely buoyed after my run with him.

My parents swivelled towards me on their bar stools at the kitchen bench, where they were eating bircher muesli side-by-side.

"Nova!" Mum exclaimed worriedly. "Oh, darling, I've got some terrible news for you."

"What? What is it Mum?" I asked, my heart pounding as I instantly started praying for all of my family to be safe – Melody, Gretchen, Veronica, and especially Veronica's kids, Arlo and Paton. I braced myself for whatever Mum was about to say.

"I've worked out why you've been losing so much weight lately," she grimaced, "and it's all my fault."

Huh? Not what I was expecting.

I took a deep soothing breath as she continued, "It's the cayenne pepper I've been putting in your morning brew. I just read an article about it online, and apparently it speeds up the metabolism."

"Seriously, Mum! That's all you're worried about? You had me completely terrified just now. I thought you were going to tell me someone had died."

"Oh, sweetheart! No! Oh, I'm so sorry. I should have thought. Are you okay?" She twitched her hands as if she was going to hug me, but then dropped them again.

"I will be, Mum. I know you're just trying to look out for me, and I do appreciate it." I patted her shoulder once before walking around the breakfast bar and into the kitchen to make my breakfast.

Mum started speaking again behind me, "It means we're going to have to stop putting cayenne pepper in your morning brew. I know it's been helping you run faster, but I really don't think you can afford to lose any more weight."

"You have my blessing to ditch the cayenne." I waved my hand with a flicking gesture as I opened the fridge. "Seriously, if I had to choose between drinking cayenne pepper and licking Satan's armpits, well, I think I'd take the armpits."

"Nova Brie! Is that how teenagers talk these days?" She turned a shocked face towards Dad, who was quietly chuckling into his coffee. "I'm clearly *far* too old for this gig." It was her favourite line whenever I said something that shocked her.

"Don't be ridic, Mum. Sixty's the new thirty, didn't you know? You're doing a great job."

"She sure is." Dad pulled Mum in for a quick side-hug from his barstool.

I grabbed all the ingredients I needed for an oat protein shake and dumped them into the blender.

"Well, thank you both." Mum smiled. "You are very kind to an old woman like me. And I do have good news for you too, Nova."

"Yeah, what's that?" I paused with my hand on the blender dial, so I'd be able to hear what she had to say.

"I'm hosting Christmas dinner here this year and all your sisters have RSVP'd that they can come. Isn't that wonderful?"

A smile tugged my cheeks upwards. "It sure is."

It gave me exactly one thing to look forward to this summer.

CHAPTER

Twenty-One

Ty was once again waiting for me on my doorstep on Tuesday morning.

"Where to, boss?" He stood up to ask as I stepped outside into the warm dark morning.

"Tangiwai Reserve?" I replied with a questioning inflection because the run would be brutal, taking us up and down the steepest parts of Laingholm Drive. Twice.

"Sure thing," he agreed, before leaping over my stairs again and taking off without waiting to see whether I followed.

Only on the return run did he let me take the lead – I guess trusting that I'd finally spent enough energy to not leave him choking on my dust. We slowed to an easy jog at the bottom of our road, and then Ty and I warmed down by stretching in his front yard next to the coop housing his flock of fluffy white chickens.

"You want to come inside for *champorado*?" Ty asked when we had finished stretching.

Past Nova would have accepted that offer in a heartbeat, but I hadn't been to his house since the day after Skye had died, two months ago. Maybe that didn't sound like such a long time in the grand scheme of things, but, in our world of popping across the road several times a day, it was at least thirty dog years. Ty still didn't know why I'd stopped hanging out with him and, even worse, his mum didn't know. I was sure to hear all about it if I suddenly showed up at Rosamie's breakfast table expecting her to feed me.

"Maybe next time," I hedged.

Ty didn't show his disappointment, but I sensed it was there. He just gave me a quirky lopsided grin, patted my back, and said, "Thanks for the run, Supernova. I'll see you tomorrow."

"Or maybe we could hang out later?" I threw it out there, all casual-like. These two days of running with him hadn't been as painful or awkward as I'd thought they'd be. I'd managed to cage my butterflies long enough to act chill around him, so maybe I could continue the act. And to be honest, being with him again was the happiest I'd been since before Skye had died.

"The boys are coming over to play video games at some point." Ty cocked his head to the side like he was gauging my reaction. "You want me to text you when they do, so we can all hang out? They've missed you."

"Yeah. Do that." I nodded. "I've missed them too."

"Great." Ty grinned.

I lifted a hand in goodbye and crossed the street back to my house, unable to keep the smile from my face.

After a shower and a hot breakfast of poached eggs on toast, I didn't know what to do with myself. I was amping to hang out with Ty and the boys again. Two months of punishing myself for loving Ty were long enough. I was over being miserable.

When Ty's text finally arrived, I was across the road and knocking on his front door within five minutes.

Matthias opened it for me. "Nova Samson, as I live and breathe!" He staggered backwards, clutching his heart like I'd stabbed him. Then he straightened up and grinned. "How is everything?"

"I'm doing alright, thanks." I made a move to squeeze past

him into the house.

"I call BS." Matthias stopped me with a hand on my shoulder and stared me down, his beady grey eyes piercing mine.

"Excuse me?" I asked, pulling my chin back.

"You've been ignoring everyone since Skye died. And don't think I haven't noticed how skinny you've gotten. You are so far from *good,* you've circled the whole galaxy and almost reached *good* again.

"Okaaaay then," I exhaled. "What do you want me to say?"

"How about... *'I'm crap, Matthias. Thanks for asking.'*"

"Man, I missed you," I said instead, stepping in to hug him and soak up his comforting presence. I had missed this so much. *Friendship.* I'd been such an idiot, cutting everyone off the way I had. What good had it even done? I'd just hurt us all.

Matthias patted my back awkwardly with his big paddle hands.

"So how are *you* doing, Matthias?" I asked, stepping out of his embrace and following him further into the house, in the direction of Ty's bedroom.

"I'm crap, Nova. Thanks for asking. Skye's gone, you're wasting away to nothing, and my man, Ty, is carrying the weight of the world on his shoulders. I'm really hoping next year turns out a bit better than this one because I don't think I can handle much more of this."

"I'm so sorry, Mattie," I said earnestly. "If there's anything I can do to help, please let me know."

It was the same useless thing people always said, so I didn't even know why it popped out of my mouth. Matthias took it for the genuine offer it was though, because, as we paused in front of Ty's open bedroom door, he said, "There is a way you could help me."

"Yeah? What's that?"

"Come surfing with us on Saturday."

I recoiled at his request. Surfing would forever be associated with Skye's last day on earth for me now. "I don't think that's such a good idea."

"Doesn't matter. That's what I'm asking." Then he added, "Ty hasn't been surfing since that day. I think it would help him to have you there."

I glanced towards Ty to check if he had heard what Matthias said. He and Peter were sitting on his bed with game controllers in their hands, and apparently he had heard because he'd thrown his head backwards against the wall and was swallowing like he was trying not to throw up.

How could I have been so selfish? All these weeks I had let Ty suffer alone, acting like my feelings about him were more important than his grief. And he had blamed himself for Skye's death because of me. There was no excuse.

"I'll get him there." I squeezed Matthias's arm. "If I have to hog-tie him and throw him over my shoulder, I'll get him there."

"Damn straight," Matthias rumbled.

CHAPTER

Twenty-Two

Like always, my alarm woke me up at 5am the next morning. I swiped it off, shoved my phone under my lavender-scented pillow, and fell straight back asleep.

It was my pillow vibrating that brought me back to consciousness a while later. Groggily, I scrambled around for my phone and pulled it out from beneath my pillow.

Ty's face lit the screen, identifying the caller. His wavy black hair was a little shorter in my photo of him than it was in reality now, but still long enough to frame his face. I was struck by the delight I saw in that old photo of him, taken pre-accident. He'd been laughing at a joke I'd told him just before I'd snapped the shot.

Back when we still told jokes.

"Hello," I spoke huskily into the phone, and then coughed to clear my throat.

"Are you seriously standing me up?" Ty demanded in my ear.

"What time is it?" I sat up and held my phone out in front of me to check the clock on the screen. "Holy cow." I pulled the phone back to my ear. "It's five-thirty! How long have you been waiting?"

"About twenty minutes."

"I'm so sorry. I'll be right out." I hung up on him and leapt out of bed, pulling on my clothes and shoes as quickly as I could. And then it hit me. The knowledge of Skye's death hadn't zapped me the very second I'd woken up. I had been so fine, I had actually fallen back asleep.

Now that I was thinking about her, my lungs burned with the loss of her friendship. But I could still *breathe,* and the urge to run wasn't compulsive like it had been for the past two months.

Racing downstairs to the kitchen, I poured Mum's brew into two cups and carried them outside to share with Ty. I grinned at the sight of him waiting patiently for me in his reflective running gear.

"Woah...." he breathed, staring at my mouth.

"What?" I asked, passing him his drink before lifting a hand self-consciously to my lips.

"Just... I really missed your smile."

"Oh." I smiled again, softer this time. "It's coming back, I guess. I didn't fall apart over Skye this morning. That's progress."

"Yeah it is." Ty nodded, taking a sip of his drink, which he immediately spat back out onto our Star Jasmine. "What the heck is this?"

"Mum's magic brew. Drink up, ya pansy. It's going to put a fire in your step like you wouldn't believe. If Mum's internet sources are to be trusted, that is."

"Brutal." He shook his head but bravely took another swig of Ma's hideous concoction.

We left our mostly full glasses sitting on my porch and then descended the stairs for our morning run.

"Where to, boss?" Ty asked me, same as every morning.

"Actually, I don't really feel like a big run today. Maybe we could just do boot camp on your front lawn instead," I suggested. Since my breathing was fine, I wasn't desperate for my normal morning run to fix me.

"Sounds good," he agreed.

We crossed our quiet street and ran drills back and forth across the Tylers' slightly sloping front lawn. Fluffy bantam hens wandered out from their coop to investigate who had so rudely awoken them before the sun had even finished rising, but squawked back under cover when our erratic motions freaked them out.

Ty dared me into a planking competition with him, timing us on his phone. I held out for four whole minutes. Ty held out for four minutes and three seconds.

"Damn it." I punched him lightly on his arm when my abs had finally stopped cramping long enough for me to sit up. "You won, you punk."

"You can't expect to be the best at everything." Ty grinned, flashing his white teeth.

"Why can't I?" I furrowed my brow at him, teasing.

"Because then nobody else would ever get the chance to impress you, ya sweat."

"I'll have you know that people impress me just fine with their humble praise and adoration," I joked. It was forever since I'd cared what anybody else thought about me, but I was starting to again. And that felt good.

"Can I ask you a question?" Ty said.

"Sure." I smiled.

"If it had been Skye driving that night and me who had died, would you have cut her off too?"

Oh, wow. Wow. Wow. Wow. He did not just ask me that.

"Nova." Ty was suddenly kneeling in front of me. "I'm sorry I asked. Just breathe, please. Breathe."

My lungs had started making a horrible rasping noise as the familiar weight of grief and guilt crushed down on my chest.

"Look at me, Nova." Ty ordered, and I painfully lifted my eyes to his, still trying to get control of my breathing without running away from him. He deserved better than that from me. After my realisation yesterday, I'd decided I was never going to run away from him again. It might help *me* cope with all of my unwanted feelings, but it was always at his expense.

"It's okay," he said. "You don't have to answer that if you don't want to. But if you ever do decide to, you've got to know that I won't be mad at you, no matter what you say. Grief doesn't always make sense. I've come to terms with that. I've just been wondering, is all, but I probably shouldn't have asked."

"No," I rasped out.

"No, what?" His normally smooth forehead wrinkled as he tried to puzzle me out. "No, I shouldn't have asked, or *no*, you wouldn't have cut Skye off?"

"No, I wouldn't have cut Skye off." I inhaled again and felt a trickle of air hit my empty lungs. "And I'm sorry I ever cut *you* off," I gasped out. "It was seriously messed up of me to do that and I'm so, sooo sorry." I inhaled again, and the sweet air reached a little deeper into my lungs this time. "I've missed you, Ty. I'm really glad you're here now – that you didn't give up on me. Is there any chance you can forgive me for leaving you to deal with Skye's death alone?"

"There's nothing to forgive." He shrugged. "You were grieving. I was the symbol of everything you'd lost. I get it." He shrugged again.

"No!" I grabbed his hand in mine and then quickly let go when I remembered I shouldn't be holding Ty's hand. "It wasn't *that*, and I shouldn't have shut you out. This horrible thing happened to you and I wasn't there for you. I should have been there. I *should* have, and I'm truly sorry I wasn't. Will you forgive me?" I asked him again.

"Of course." He grinned, shaking his head at my insistence we do this apology properly. "Of course, I forgive you, Nova. I just want you to be happy again. I thought respecting your space was the way to go, but when I saw you shrinking away week by week, I decided I'd left you alone too long. And for that, *I'm* sorry. Can you ever forgive me?"

"This is getting ridiculous." I smiled, finally inhaling to the very back of my lungs. Oxygen had never tasted so sweet. It was almost as sweet as my oldest friend, sitting beside me, still caring about me even after everything I'd done. "But yes, I forgive you. Even though there's nothing to forgive, I do."

"So, we're cool?" He stuck out his hand for me to shake.

I took it and shook it firmly up and down. I tried to let it go, but he just grabbed it harder and darted his other hand forward to tickle me under my armpit.

"You jerk!" I squirmed out of his grasp and jumped away because I was terribly ticklish. Which he *knew*.

"Come back," he implored. "I swear I won't tickle you again."

Cautiously, I made my way back to him, getting ready to dart away if I needed to, but he kept his word. He didn't touch me again, just dropped down onto his back on the grass.

I lay down beside him, and together we rested on his soft lawn under the ever-brightening sky, just being there in the moment and breathing dawn's crisp air. It felt like my missing half had been returned to me.

I watched the clouds drift overhead and thought of my God, who I had ignored far too often while I wallowed in self-pity, and I apologised to him too in my head.

"Please forgive me, Lord, for turning my back on you. Thank you for bringing Ty back into my life, despite my terrible decision to cut him off. Thank you for bringing peace between me and Mum. Comfort me and Ty as we grieve over Skye. Help me figure out how to keep on living, even though she's gone. Help me to be the friend Ty needs. In Jesus' name. Amen."

CHAPTER
Twenty-Three

Peter texted me early Saturday morning: *Surf report's good. Waiting outside with Mattie. You're up.*

Translation: *Get Ty's arse out here.*

My one and only job was to get Ty out of his house and into Peter's car.

Ty hadn't driven since the accident that had killed Skye. Even though he'd kept his licence in the end and had even had a new car show up in his driveway, I'd never once seen it move.

If Matthias was to be believed, Ty also hadn't been surfing since that night, and apparently only I had the power to convince him to try it again. Which meant knocking on his front door and facing up to Rosamie Tyler, Ty's tiny, but fiercely protective mother.

I stashed my wetsuit and other gear in Peter's car and left him and Matthias to tie my surfboard to the roof racks. Peter had also brought a spare board for Ty, since his one had been destroyed in the crash.

As I walked past Ty's carport towards his house, I jumped up to tap his basketball hoop for good luck. Then I knocked timidly on the Tylers' glass front door. So timidly, nobody heard me or came to answer.

I rapped against the glass pane again, louder this time. Still no answer. Why was I even knocking? Ty's house was like my second home. I decided to re-stake my claim on it and open the front door.

"Hello," I bellowed. Nobody responded.

"Hello," I called again as I walked through the living room and into the hallway that led to Ty's bedroom.

His door was shut when I got there, but I knocked on it softly. Again, no answer.

Pushing the door open, I walked into Ty's darkened bedroom. His blackout curtains were pulled closed, so I could barely make out his form on the bed. As my eyes adjusted to the low light, I realised that although his room wasn't messy by most boys' standards, it *was* messy by Ty's. He'd left dirty clothes dropped on the floor, and there were half a dozen empty protein shakes on his rimu side table and tallboy.

"Ty," I whispered, as I sat down beside him and placed a hand on his shoulder. "It's time to wake up."

His eyes sprung open and he flipped onto his back, then launched into a sitting position, pulling his dark grey duvet up with him.

I leapt off his bed at this sudden flurry of movement.

"What are you doing here?" he asked me, wild-eyed. "Did I miss our morning run?"

"Nope. It's the holidays. No running on weekends. Today, we're going surfing." I gave him my most winning smile. After two years of corrective braces in my early teens, my smile was pretty killer.

But Ty just groaned and fell backwards. "I already told the guys that I'm not interested."

"Too bad," I enunciated. "Because I need a surfing partner and think you'd be perfect for the job."

He groaned at my echo of the line he'd used to convince me

to run with him, but then looked up at me from beneath sooty lashes. "So this is payback, is it?"

"Payback? No. Don't be salty. Let's just say I'm returning the favour. You did a good thing, foisting yourself on me every morning. You brought me back. Now I'm here to remind *you* that life's still worth living. And there's no better place to remind you of that than staring down the face of a six-foot wave."

"Six-foot, eh?" he considered me. "Is that the official surf report or are you just waxing poetic?"

"Check for yourself. Six-footers are rolling in at Piha as we speak."

He blinked when I said, "Piha," but rallied himself and stood up. "Give me a minute to get dressed and I'll be right out. Who's driving?"

"Peter. He's waiting for us outside with Matthias."

"*Of course* he is. You're all first-class jerks, you know that, right?"

"Yes. Yes, we are." I smiled. "But you love us for it."

"Sad, but true." He shoved me with his shoulder. "Now get outside, unless you want to stay and watch me strip."

"Gross!" I exclaimed. "No thanks. That would be like watching my brother strip, if I had a brother." Lies. Terrible lies. But it was safer to talk about him like a brother and keep some necessary distance between us so that I could remember my place in his life.

"Yeah, yeah. I'm the brother you never had," he rumbled, pushing me out of his bedroom and closing the door behind me.

I rushed back through the house to tell Peter and Matthias the excellent news – that I'd convinced Ty to come – but pulled up short when I saw Ty's parents eating breakfast in the dining room.

"Oh. Hey, Rosamie. Hey, James. How are you both?"

This was awkward.

They jumped to their feet, and, although they physically couldn't have looked more different from each other – short, curvy, and dark-haired compared to tall, lean, and grey-haired, they shared identical expressions of delight.

"We're better for seeing you, darling girl." Rosamie choked on a sob as she darted forward and pulled me into an embrace. Like Mr Tyler, I also towered over her, so I ended up inhaling the usual lungful of jasmine-scented hair, but it was worth it. She didn't hate me after all.

And then she lightly smacked my bottom and had me re-thinking that last assessment.

"Where have you been, Nova Pie?" she asked with a scowl that belied the sweetness of her nickname for me. "I keep asking Andrew to bring you around to see us, but he refuses. He deserves a smacked bottom too. Tell me what I did to raise such a naughty boy?"

Great. Now I'd managed to get Ty in trouble.

"That's not true, Rosamie. You raised a good Catholic boy. You know you did."

"Hmmm, hmmm," she replied with her hands on her hips, unconvinced.

"I've just been sad, is all. I didn't want to see anyone until recently. But then your very good, very well-raised son forced me out of my shell, so please don't be mad at him."

"Oh, hush, as if I could ever be mad at that gorgeous face of his." She swatted me on my arm and then headed into the kitchen. "How about I cook *spamsilog* for breakfast? Let him know just how proud of him I am."

"Ah, actually, can he take a raincheck on that?" I stammered. "He doesn't have time for a cooked breakfast this morning. Our friends are waiting outside to take us surfing."

"Oh, hush," she whistled in annoyance again. But she soon cheered up when she pulled the lid off a pot on the stove and said,

"Well he can at least make time for champorado. He shouldn't go surfing on an empty stomach."

"Yes, of course," I replied. "I'm sure he'd appreciate that."

"You too," she ordered, slapping a huge serving of chocolate rice into a ceramic bowl for me. "You don't look so good, Nova Pie. Way too skinny. You need fattening up."

And that's how Ty found me chowing down on champorado when he emerged from his bedroom in a pair of maroon board shorts and a fresh white t-shirt. His black hair was falling forward across his forehead and he had a canvas backpack slung over one broad shoulder.

"What's this?" he asked me. "I've been inviting you for champorado all week with no success, yet one request from my ma and you're eating it like a docile little puppy."

"Well…," I said, "I like your ma."

"Ohhhhhh, burn." He slapped his thigh before grabbing the bowl his mother held out to him and sliding into the rimu seat next to mine. His deodorant's clean scent wafted over me, as well as another smell – something delicious and unique to Ty. "How long do you think Peter and Matthias are going to wait for us out there?"

"All day, I reckon."

"Should we see how long we can push it?" He smirked at me.

"We could…" I grinned, warming dangerously under that bright smile of his, "but those six-footers aren't going to surf themselves."

"You're right." Ty jumped back to his feet and bent down to kiss his mum on her head. "I'm taking this to go, Nanay," he told her. "Waves to catch." Then he bolted out the front door, breakfast in hand.

CHAPTER
Twenty-Four

Our excitement about the surfing trip dimmed a little on the drive to Piha, when Ty pointed out the site of the crash. It was marked by a white cross covered in flowers, and the tree behind it showed signs of damage from the accident. Peter slowed the car as we drove past, and I cried softly as I was struck afresh by how Skye had died.

We didn't talk much after that. Peter turned up the volume on the car stereo to fill the emptiness instead.

It was almost 8am when we finally descended the steep, winding hill to Piha. Thankfully, my mood couldn't help but lift at the sight of Lion Rock jutting out proudly from the centre of Piha's black sand beach. Ty and I were both sitting in the backseat of Peter's four-wheel drive, but, when I turned to share my joy with him, I found him doing that swallowing thing again with his eyes squeezed tight.

I leaned across the seat, placed my hand on his warm forearm, and said the first thing that came to mind, "It's a beautiful day to start living."

"Yeah it is," he whispered, although his eyes remained closed.

I unclasped my seatbelt so I could slide into the middle seat, where I quickly fastened the lap-belt before leaning my head against his shoulder. "I know this is hard, but you're the best person I know – and the best surfing partner I could ask for." I was doing my best to cheer him up like he'd cheered me up in recent days.

"You know it." He shifted his head until he was looking down at me. I returned his gaze. At least I'd gotten him to open his eyes, which had little flecks of gold lighting up the brown. Almost like stars. "What?" he whispered, and I realised I'd been staring a little too directly into those star-speckled eyes of his.

"Oh, sorry." I turned my head to give him space, like a normal person.

"No seriously, what were you just thinking?" He nudged my shoulder.

"Ah," I stammered. "Your eyes are just really striking. I never noticed it before, but they kind of look like they're filled with stars."

"Well, they're a'ight, I guess." He smiled. "But I like stormy blue eyes better."

Like mine? I wondered because, despite her name, Skye's eyes had been brown. Nothing stormy blue about them. I shook my head stupidly, my heart hammering way too loudly in my chest. Ty could probably hear it; we were sitting that close. What was I doing? Skye should be sitting next to Ty, not me.

"You've gone awfully quiet," Ty murmured.

"Oh, sorry." I swallowed my guilt. "Just thinking about Skye. She would've loved coming here today."

He didn't flinch, thank goodness, just turned to look sadly out of his window towards the car park we were pulling into. "I don't think she would've loved it as much as you think she would've," he finally said.

"What do you mean?" I asked.

"Nothing." He turned back to me, a smile pulling tight across his face. "Forget I said anything."

"Not likely," I muttered to myself.

It was a weird day after that. The good summer surf had drawn droves of surfers to the beach, so we spent the morning vying for positions on the waves, which I hated. Naturally, I wanted to be polite and let people go in front of me, but as soon as the male surfers saw I was a girl, they made way for me like I'd get smashed if they got too close. It was nice, in a gentlemanly kind of way I guess, but it also made me feel like I was taking up way more than my fair share of space. I felt compelled to go all out to prove I could surf just as well as any guy, taking risks I wouldn't normally have taken after a two-month hiatus from the surf.

Yeah, I got pummelled.

But I didn't let that stop me, and I pretty quickly mastered my board again. I'd been surfing since I was a kid, and that muscle memory hadn't deserted me. Maybe just my nerve, although I was clawing that back with Matthias showing off beside me.

He dropped down into a wave on my right and I hooted for him as he leapt to his feet and switched up and down its face. I caught the next wave, carving it up like Sunday roast. I wasn't sure where Peter or Ty were amongst the army of black wetsuits, but trusted they were looking out for each other. Surfing was fun but dangerous, especially on New Zealand's West Coast. It was marginally safer with friends.

We spent a good couple of hours out in the water before calling it quits. Matthias and I made our way onto shore, shucking off our ankle ropes once we reached the beach and heading towards the dry bit of hot black sand where we'd left our gear. Peter found us snacking on grapes 20 minutes later. He was carrying two boards.

"Where's Ty?" I asked, worriedly.

"He went for a walk up Lion Rock." Peter gestured towards the formidable stone that effectively split Piha into two beaches.

"Oh." My heartbeat returned to normal as I looked up, trying to make out Ty's form, but he wasn't anywhere I could see on the winding path.

"He didn't want company?" I asked.

"Maybe," Peter said, "but I'm stuffed after surfing. I want to lie down for a bit and warm up." Which he did, right there on the beach, getting his spiky black hair full of sand.

"Well, I'd be keen for a walk," I said to no one in particular. I felt jittery with excitement as I got to my feet. The two hours of surfing without seeing Ty had felt way too long. I had already changed back into denim shorts and a green tee, but I now slid a pair of jandals onto my feet for the climb. "You wanna come, Matthias?" I asked, not because I wanted him to come, but because I knew I should be trying to provide buffers between my feelings and Ty. The more time I spent with Ty, the harder it was to remind myself to respect Skye's memory.

"Nah, that sounds like hard work." Matthias threw a grape into the air and snapped it between his teeth. "I'll just hang here with Pete. See you on the flip side."

"Okay." I nodded, more excited than I should have been as I headed off towards the well-trodden path that wound steeply up Lion Rock. I was a hopeless case. After avoiding Ty for two months, I physically couldn't make myself do it any longer.

I found Ty beneath the watchful eyes of a beautiful *pou whenua*. He sat on a stone bench that curved into the hillside, cocooned by glossy green flax bushes. He'd folded his wetsuit down at the waist, so his muscular torso was bare and glowing golden in the sunlight.

Just breathe.

"Hey." I walked closer and crouched down in front of him. "I hope I'm not interrupting."

"Never," he replied, and his voice was husky like he had been crying.

"You alright?" I asked him.

"I've been better." His breath hitched.

I put a hand on his bare shoulder to comfort him as I sat down beside him. He fell sideways onto my lap, almost knocking me over as he wrapped his sun-warmed arms around me and cried without making a noise, exactly like he had the morning after the accident. I ran my fingers through his damp hair and murmured nonsense words into the top of his head, grateful to finally be there for him, even if the close contact was ripping my heart to shreds.

Ty's shuddering slowly eased as he cried himself out.

"Sorry about that." He eventually pushed himself back up to a sitting position and roughly rubbed at his wet face with his palms.

"You've got nothing to be sorry about," I assured him, rubbing circles on his back. "Your girlfriend died. You're allowed to cry whenever and as much as you want."

"I miss her," he whispered. "And I feel so guilty. You have no idea. I'm racked with guilt over it."

"It wasn't your fault," I gently reminded him. "Accidents happen, *especially* on winding country roads."

"I know they do. But you weren't there, and it was my fault. I was distracted. I should've been more careful."

I figured he was just being hard on himself, so I said, "Guilt is pointless. It's just going to make you feel rotten about something you can't change. And I know I didn't help with the guilt-thing, ignoring you for two months like I did, but you've got to believe me – that had nothing to do with me blaming you. I *never* blamed you."

"You're sure?" Ty locked his teary gaze on me, checking I was being straight with him. He must've seen the truth behind my eyes though because he nodded. Once. Twice. "Okay then. I'll do my best to learn to live with it. I can't promise you I'll be back to my old self anytime soon, but I'll work on it."

"I don't need the old you back." I patted his wetsuit-clad knee. "The old you wouldn't have opened up to me like this. The old you wouldn't have let himself cry in front of me. And the old you wouldn't have understood why I've been acting like such a head case since Skye died. We've both changed, but I think that's a good thing."

"Thank you for being here, Nova." He eased himself to his feet and then held out a hand to pull me up too. "One day at a time."

"We've got this." I nodded in agreement as his strong hand clasped mine, and I tried to ignore how good it felt.

CHAPTER
Twenty-Five

Even though I didn't *need* to get up at dawn for my morning run over the summer holidays, I kept at it to beat the heat and commuter traffic. After the first couple of weeks of running with Ty, I started going slightly easier on us by setting my alarm for 6am instead of 5am.

Ty was half keeping me sane, half driving me to insanity with his insistence on running with me whenever I did. Every morning, faithful as man's best friend, he was there waiting for me on my doorstep, forgoing his opportunity to sleep in.

And every morning, I lit up in his presence even though the part of me that was loyal to Skye felt ashamed that I did.

Andrew Tyler, first thing in the morning, was a beautiful sight to behold. Still rumpled from sleep, with hooded eyes and crease lines on his face, he eased into a long loping run in front of me, and I couldn't keep my eyes off him. Some people have goofy running gaits, toes pointed in odd directions or arms flailing weirdly. Not Ty. He made it look effortless – his body in perfect alignment with itself. Did he watch me when I ran? I told myself it didn't matter, but I knew I cared.

And then, because we started our days together, we invariably made plans for later in the day too – plans that usually included

Peter, Matthias, and the great outdoors.

"You wanna go to Kitekite Falls this afternoon?" Ty asked me as we stretched in his front yard after a brutal run up The Little Muddy Creek Walkway.

"I wouldn't mind going swimming there," I replied. "It feels like today's going to be a hot one."

"What sort of bikini do you wear for swimming under a waterfall?" Ty asked as he bent forward into a stretch.

"What?" I gaped at him. Why was he thinking about me in a bikini?

"Don't you have some sort of rating system for your togs?" he clarified, grinning at my stunned expression. "I just wondered if that system covered waterfalls."

"Oh…" He'd been making a joke. Of course. "Yeah, definitely no string bikinis allowed near waterfalls. Or near Matthias," I added as an afterthought.

"He wouldn't," Ty growled.

"Nah, he wouldn't. It's just my secret fear because he complained so much about missing out on The Great Bikini Incident."

"Ha. Yeah, he did." Ty chuckled ruefully. "But to be fair, he was 13 at the time. He's grown up a lot since then."

"I know, and I trust him. Really, I do. He was just *so* disappointed when he first heard about it."

"Yeah, he was. Man, I'm glad he wasn't there that day."

"Aren't we all?" I shuddered.

"I do apologise for my dodgy friend." Ty grimaced. "Would you rather go to the falls without him and Pete?"

"Nah, invite them. Mattie's turned into a decent human being." Besides, I didn't trust myself to go swimming alone at a beautiful waterfall with Ty. *I* was not such a good person.

"Cool," Ty said. "I'll see if Pete can drive us. I'll text you when we're ready to go. Probably around lunchtime."

"Okay, cool. I'll pack a picnic."

"Sweet." He did that chin-lift thing guys do, and we parted ways to head into our own homes.

Up in my bathroom, I took a ridiculously long shower so I could wash my too-long hair and shave everywhere that might be exposed by my togs. My mind kept flicking back to Ty's bikini question. It made me want to look amazing at Kitekite Falls, even though I was crossing into dangerous territory with that line of thinking. Could I dare to wear a bikini?

I pulled out all of my togs from my chest of drawers and laid them on my bed. There was my super-safe *Speedo* one-piece, a black bikini with padded push up cups that gave me the illusion of breasts, and a tiny emerald green bikini that I only ever wore to sunbathe – maximising vitamin D and minimising tan lines. Which one?

I looked at them all, but my eyes kept fixating on the emerald green one. It was the one I wanted to wear.

My mum would say this was a terrible idea. She was big on modesty, which was totally understandable to me now. Melody used to push the boundaries with her outfits all the time, wearing super short shorts and crop tops until Mum sat her down and had a long talk with her about it. I could finally guess what Mum had told her. It had a big impact on Melody, who embraced Mum's way of thinking and quickly became the poster girl for beautiful modesty. She'd made a good side hustle out of it too with her blog and YouTube channel. Lots of people were sick of the way girls got over-sexualised in the media. Melody promoted a refreshing alternative, embracing all that was beautiful about the feminine form without overexposing it.

I couldn't think about that today though.

My feelings for Ty were only growing stronger by the day, and I was itching to know whether he could see me as anything more than a friend. If I wore the green bikini, and he didn't even notice, then I could safely spend time with him without ever worrying about something more happening between us.

No chance of disloyalty to Skye if only one of the players was interested.

However, if he did show interest in me, then I had a decision to make about how to respond. My head and my heart were at war on this one, but I had a feeling I knew which one would eventually win out.

Without second-guessing myself, I put on the green bikini. Decision made. Let the chips fall where they may. It was time to find out whether Ty could even look at me with more than brotherly affection.

CHAPTER

Twenty-Six

We traipsed the 20-minute track to Kitekite Falls listening to Matthias's newly-minted summer playlist. He blasted it from a portable speaker he'd tucked into a drink bottle pocket on the side of his backpack. Only Matthias would think he could improve on the natural sounds of birds, cicadas, and a babbling stream.

Ty carried his prized *Canon* camera on a strap around his neck and was lost in capturing every bird, nīkau palm, kauri tree, and fern.

"Check this out, Nova." Ty stopped our walk so he could show me an amazing photo he'd taken of a tui in flight, its blue wings catching a ray of sunlight streaming through the trees.

"Oh, wow." I breathed. "It's stunning, Ty. This is going straight to the pool room." I added that last bit in an Australian accent.

"Yeah, I reckon." Ty chuckled, catching my reference to the movie *The Castle*.

I made him show Peter and Matthias too, and they *ooohed* and *aaahed* appropriately. Then we resumed our hike, which followed the river under the shade of lush native trees.

When we finally arrived at the foot of the majestic falls, we set up our picnic on the rocky ground in front of the swimming hole. Not strictly comfortable, but we found the smoothest rocks we could and laid out our towels on them. I'd made chicken and roast capsicum ciabatta rolls, as well as chocolate brownies to share, but before I could even pull them out of my backpack, Ty placed his offering of trail mix into the middle, Matthias ripped open a bag of *Twisties* and screwed the cap off a 1.5 litre bottle of *L&P*, and Peter took the lid off a round thermos of dumplings.

"Oh, yum!" I exclaimed when I saw the dumplings. "Did you make them yourself?"

"Don't be ridiculous." He laughed. "Do you even know how long it takes to make dumplings? I bought them from the Chinese takeaways shop in Glen Eden and put them in this thermos so you'd *think* I made them."

"I don't care who made them." Matthias reached for the thermos. "I just want them in my belly."

When I tried to reach for a dumpling, Matthias smacked my hand away. "You won't like it," he assured me before shovelling three dumplings into his mouth.

"Let the lady eat a dumpling," Ty commanded, "or I'll sit on your face."

"That's what she said," Matthias said and then chuckled.

The rest of us groaned. But at least thanks to Ty running interference, I managed to get my hands on one pork dumpling before they all disappeared. I then pulled out the neatly packaged rolls and brownies from my bag and set them in the middle of our circle.

"Now you're just trying to make me feel guilty," Matthias complained.

"Would I do that?" I asked him, smiling.

Peter crammed a brownie into his mouth and said, "These are next level, Noves."

At least, I think that's what he said. It was hard to tell around his mouthful of food.

"She's just flexing on us." Matthias rolled his eyes, but I

noticed that didn't stop him grabbing a piece.

Ty unwrapped one of the ciabatta rolls and said, "These are legit, Nova. Did you make them?"

"Nah, I bought them from the bakery in Glen Eden."

"Seriously?" Ty checked my face to gauge whether I was being sarcastic.

"Not seriously." I shook my head, laughing. "I made them myself."

"Well my stomach loves you for it," Ty said.

And I'm not going to mention what my stomach did at Ty's casual use of the L-word. Suffice it to say that it was difficult for me to finish my chicken roll, and I didn't even bother with a brownie.

After we'd finished eating, Peter, Matthias, and I relaxed on our towels, listening to Matthias's playlist. Only Ty couldn't sit still. He was too busy snapping photos of us from different angles, using the waterfall as our backdrop. And then he set the timer on his camera so that he could jump into one of the photos too. Only when he was finally happy with his photographic evidence of the day, did he pack up his camera and reclaim his seat on the towel next to mine.

I had been distracted by Ty's camera antics, so hadn't noticed till now, but Matthias's summer playlist wasn't as upbeat as usual. It was filled with depressing ballads and songs of struggles and heartache. I started to wonder if everything was okay with him.

"How are you doing these days?" I asked Matthias, leaning my elbows on my knees to give him my full attention.

"Ah... not so good." Matthias shrugged, not quite meeting my gaze. "Mum's having another flare up."

"Oh, stink," I commiserated. His mum had Multiple Sclerosis. Most of the time it didn't give her too much trouble, but every now and then she had a flare up that caused numbness in various parts of her body. "How long has it been going on this time?"

"About a month." He sighed. "I think she's been doing too much."

"What's she been doing?" Ty asked.

"Trying to sell our house." Matthias shrugged like he was trying to play down embarrassment. "Dad's business isn't doing real good, so Mum's stressed about money. She keeps talking about downsizing to reduce our mortgage, but the house needs lots of work to get it market-worthy, and she doesn't think she can afford to pay anyone to do it. I'm pretty sure she was planning to do it all by herself, before this latest episode hit."

"What kind of work does your place need?" I asked.

"What doesn't it need?" Matthias chuckled ruefully, shaking his head. "I think Mum was going to focus on painting and landscaping though, so it looks good for the photos."

"I'd be happy to help out," I offered. "I've got nothing better to do these holidays."

"Yeah, me too," Ty agreed.

"Man… Guys…. That's cool of you to offer," Matthias stammered, "but you seriously don't need to do that. I mean, we wouldn't be able to pay you or anything."

"Doesn't matter." I shook my head and shrugged my shoulders. "Seriously. Put me to work. I kind of need something to focus on right now."

"I'm with her." Ty pointed my way. "Happy to volunteer. Although, I notice you're awfully quiet over there, Liu." He levelled a stare at Peter.

Peter dropped his head into his hands and asked his knees, "Why do all my friends have to be such lads? I had the perfect summer of chill lined up."

"Mate." Matthias patted him on his shoulder. "Don't let these Muppets force you into doing anything you don't want to do. Enjoy your summer."

"Of course, I have to help. Otherwise I'll be the lame friend who sat on his admittedly fine arse all summer while his friends slaved away for a good cause."

"Hey! I'm not a charity case." Matthias's grey eyes sparked as his heavy forehead drew down over them. He shoved his *L&P* bottle back into his backpack and loudly zipped the bag closed.

"You're not the charity case here." I assured him, leaning forward to pat his knee. "*I* am. I NEED this or I'll shake loose of my skin."

Ty nodded in agreement. "So that's settled then. We'll help however we can. You just say the word and we'll be there. But for now, who's up for a swim?"

"Me," I replied instantly, remembering my earlier plan. This could be my moment. All I had to do was take off my top and leggings and let nature take its course. Of course, now mortification was taking over. I wish I had even a handful of Skye's confidence. Why, *oh why*, had I decided to wear my smallest bikini?

To delay the inevitable while I built up my nerve, I took my time packing up our picnic things. The guys all shucked off their shoes and t-shirts without a second thought. Ty wore mustard board shorts that somehow made his tanned skin look even more luminous than normal. I barely noticed what the other guys wore, but they were already stepping from rock to rock towards the swimming hole when I finally stood up and took off my pants and top. I pulled out my hair-tie, slipping it onto my wrist as I let my long hair fall loosely around my shoulders, hoping for the Eve-in-the-Garden effect.

Ty yelled over his shoulder, "You coming, Nova?" and then stiffened as he turned to face me fully. His eyes widened when he took in the sight of me in my skimpy bikini.

Unfortunately, I can only describe the expression on his face as one of abject horror.

CHAPTER

Twenty-Seven

Ty came storming out of the waterhole towards me so fast, I took a stumbling step backwards. He grabbed my hand and yelled back to the others, "Nova and I are going swimming up top. See ya later." He then pulled me swiftly up the rocks and onto the gravel track that led to the top of the waterfall.

"What are you doing?" I whispered angrily as we started climbing. His reaction had not been what I was hoping for, and now I felt like crying.

"What are *you* doing?" he angry-whispered back. "You told me yourself you were worried about wearing a bikini around Matthias, and here you are in the skimpiest thing I've ever seen."

"You're rescuing me?" I smiled as sudden understanding dawned.

"Trying to."

"I don't need rescuing." I pulled my hand out of his grasp and stopped our ascent. "I told you it was my secret fear, not that he would actually do anything dodgy."

"Well… maybe I don't want him and Peter looking at you and getting any funny ideas."

"What kind of funny ideas?"

"You know what kind," he growled, staring grimly through the trees ahead.

"You've really got this overprotective older brother thing down, don't you?" I asked, daring him to contradict me.

Ty turned to face me then. He stared directly into my eyes for several seconds without dropping his gaze to my bikini-clad body. Then he arched one perfect black eyebrow and said, "I am *not* your brother."

"I know you're not," I replied softly, heart *racing.*

"Sure about that?" He arched that eyebrow even higher and pulled his mouth into a disbelieving line that turned the scar on his chin white.

"One hundred percent sure." I nodded emphatically. "I don't have a brother."

"Okay then." He nodded, although he still looked serious and scary as heck.

"Do you think we could go swimming now?" I asked in a voice that tried not to squeak.

"Yeah. But we're still swimming up top."

"Fine by me," I agreed and moved to lead the way up the narrow path. If he wanted to keep me to himself, I was okay with that. I still needed to figure out how he saw me. Apparently, *not* as his sister.

Ty stopped me again with a hand on my shoulder and said, "I'll lead."

"What's your obsession with always being in front?" I asked him.

"You really want me to follow you? In *that* bikini?" He shook his head in exasperation. "I'm trying to be a gentleman here."

Huh. I hadn't thought of that. "Fine. You lead."

"Thank you."

We were both sweating and had more than a few stone bruises on our feet by the time we got to the top of the winding track, but it was so worth it when we stopped to take in the breathtaking sight of the first aquamarine waterhole. I knew from past visits that this waterhole led to several more, which tumbled down in a series of shallow drops before falling off the edge of the cliff and disappearing into the green valley below where the boys were swimming. From where we stood, we could only see the first waterhole, although it was still completely stunning.

"Wow," I breathed. "I'd forgotten how beautiful this place is."

"It's next level." Ty nodded slowly. "Let's do this again. Before the summer's over, let's come back here."

"Yes! I'd totally be up for that."

Ty nodded and then moved ahead of me to the ledge overlooking the waterhole. Without even pausing, he cannonballed in. When he surfaced, he swam forward to the other end so I could jump in too, but I waited for him to turn around before descending to the ledge. I wanted him to watch me so I could get a sense of the thoughts behind his gaze.

Of course, as soon as his eyes were on me, I became completely self-conscious and aware of all the different body parts I somehow needed to coordinate. My hands had never felt so twitchy or full of fingers before. I stopped at the ledge above the waterhole and took a moment to gather myself, using my jittery fingers to braid my hair over my left shoulder and secure it with the hair-tie I had pulled out earlier.

That done, my hands flitted out nervously again – but I bravely lined up my toes with the edge of the ledge and looked directly into Ty's gaze.

He was watching me with half-slit eyes, but I couldn't read the expression in them.

I sucked my bottom lip into my mouth, holding it there with my teeth as I tried to read something in his expression. I didn't know. Didn't know. *Didn't know.*

"Count me in," I finally broke the silence.

"Okay. On three," Ty replied in a low gravelly voice. "One… Two… Three."

With a deep breath, I launched myself into the pool, head going under briefly before I could push off the bottom and spring back up.

"Jiminy Cricket! It's cold," I spluttered when my head re-emerged, gasping as my previously overheated skin reacted against the frigid water.

Laughing huskily, Ty said, "Come here. We'll move to the next pool down. It'll be warmer in the sunshine."

My entire body instantly overheated again as I glided through the water towards him. We were alone, but if anyone was watching us, they'd probably think we were a couple. Would Ty ever want that? Was Skye watching us from heaven and hating me right now? Was there even anything to hate, or were all these raw feelings completely one-sided?

When I reached Ty's side, he held out a hand to help me up onto the rocks. My palm tingled at the contact, but as soon as we were both stable, he let it go so he could carefully edge his way down the slippery rocks into the next smaller rock pool. I followed behind him, leaving a decent amount of space so I wouldn't take him down with me if I slipped. Once we were both back in the water, we found a space at the front of the pool where we could crouch down and rest our arms on the rock ledge, our shoulders warming in the sunshine. I took in the sight of the tree-filled valley and sighed in awe. Its beauty distracted me until Ty's shoulder knocked into mine and reminded me all over again of who I was here with.

"How's this?" Ty asked, looking down at me from under his long lashes. "Any better?"

"Yeah. This is… perfect," I said.

Perfect, except now I was completely on edge crouching next to Ty in that isolated spot. Any second he was going to make a move, or say something, or do something.

Any second now.

But we just soaked in the pool for a bit, and then I turned around to look at the water rushing down from the pool above us. Ty also turned around... and looked at the rushing water.

I was dying cell by cell.

All of these feelings were jittering around inside of me like I was a shaken-up bottle of ginger beer, and I knew that my self-control had reached its limit. Staying away from Ty had truly been my only option for respecting Skye's memory because now, sitting beside him in this stunning secluded spot, I was ready to throw my guilt-induced self-restraint right over the edge of the waterfall.

All Ty had to do was make a move. That's all he had to do. But either he wasn't picking up on the signals I was putting out, or he was... and he wasn't interested.

Maybe he expected me to make the first move. I mean, I had just ignored him for two months without any explanation. But seriously, did he not realise that of the two of us, I was the one with zero relationship experience, whereas he'd spent an entire year kissing my best friend?

Maybe that was it. Maybe he was still thinking about Skye. Maybe he wasn't thinking about me at all. Maybe I was an idiot.

He finally broke the silence as we turned back around to look out over the valley. "There's something I've been meaning to apologise for."

"Oh yeah?" I asked in surprise. "What's that?"

"I'm really sorry that Skye and I started dating on your birthday," he said. "If I had known we were going to get together, I would have picked any other day to do it."

"What do you mean, *if* you had known?" I said. "You asked her out!"

"No, I didn't." Ty shook his head.

"Yes, you did!" I exclaimed, frustrated. "You slow-danced with her, then leaned in and asked her to go out with you. She said, 'yes' and kissed you, and then you both came back to the table and…"

"If I had asked Skye out, which I definitely didn't, do you really think I would've chosen to do it on your 16th birthday? Skye might've been *your* best friend, Nova, but you've always been *mine*. Don't you think I would've had the decency to choose any other freakin' day of the year? I mean, look what happened this year? You had to move your whole birthday party just so Skye and I could celebrate our anniversary."

"I don't understand." My shoulders were shaking. "What are you saying? What really happened at my 16th?"

Ty flicked water off his forehead and met my eyes fleetingly before gazing back out over the waterfall and saying, "We were all dancing and having a good time. After a few songs, the boys went to sit down, and I saw Skye signalling for you to sit down too. I tried to get you to stay, but you smiled at me and Skye like you were rooting for us to get together. And then you left, without even a backward glance. I danced one more song with Skye to be polite, but didn't like that we were ignoring you on your birthday, so, when the song finished, I asked her if she wanted to sit down too. The next thing I knew, she was smiling and pulling me down for a kiss. I was pretty stunned, I tell ya. I was even more stunned when she dragged me back to the table and told you all I'd just asked her out. I would've set the record straight right then, but everyone looked so happy for us. I didn't have the heart to embarrass her, so I just went along with it."

"For a whole year?" I squeaked, my hands forming fists under the water.

"Well, as it turned out, we worked as a couple, so I guess I got lucky with that."

I was stunned by his revelation. And I felt sick to the stomach as I remembered Skye's excited diary entry from that night. How had she gotten it so wrong?

"I think I hate you a little bit for this." I glared at him.

"Why?" Ty's eyes widened.

"Because," I spluttered. "I don't know. She loved you! But you were with her by accident. That's messed up."

"Well, if it was a messed up situation," he shrugged, "I like to think I made the best of it."

"You don't understand." I kneaded my hands together. "She was head-over-heels, red-*M&Ms* in love with you."

Ty sighed. "I know. And look where it got her."

CHAPTER

Twenty-Eight

Mum drove me and Ty to Matthias's house on Thursday morning for our first official work day. It was a quiet ride.

I didn't know what to think about Ty's revelation. On one hand, I felt sad for Skye that her relationship with Ty hadn't come about in a totally genuine way. On the other hand, I felt like she'd somehow manipulated Ty into going out with her, and if she hadn't, I wouldn't have had the torturous year I'd had watching them date each other.

Ty confused me too. Why didn't he just set her straight right when it happened? Maybe he'd gone along with it to see where it would lead, or maybe he had always been secretly hoping for something to happen with Skye.

Still in my own thoughts, I drifted past Ty towards the Smiths' backyard. And then I stopped in my tracks when I realised the size of the job we had signed up for. Both the house and yard were enormous but rundown – as if none of the Smiths had done any maintenance on the place since they'd bought it. Understandable, with a sick mum and a stressed-out dad.

A concrete tennis court stood on the right-hand side of the back lawn, where it was slowly being overtaken by Kikuyu grass. An empty, rectangular, in-ground pool dominated the left-hand side of the lawn. There were no gardens, decks, or patios to speak of – just lots and lots of Kikuyu.

Peter hadn't shown up yet, and Matthias was still inside, so I turned around to survey the massive two-story house. It was brick on the bottom level, which was good news because at least that didn't require any maintenance (besides a good water-blast to get the lichen off), but the top level was a painted stucco that had lost most of its yellow paint. I didn't even want to look inside the house to see what kind of state that was in. We already had enough work in front of us to last the summer.

A *Twenty-One Pilots* song came drifting out of the house, and Ty walked up to stand beside me. The sound grew louder as Matthias emerged through a set of French doors from his living room, a portable speaker tucked into the side pocket of his cargo shorts. "Hey guys," he said to us. "Thanks for coming."

"No worries, bro," Ty replied.

"So..." I knocked my fists together in a *let's do this* gesture. "What's the game plan?"

"To be honest," Matthias replied, "I don't have a clue. I asked Mum and she was super vague. Seems like she hasn't got all the gear we need to do much of anything."

"What does she have?" Ty asked.

"A couple of buckets of paint, paint brushes, and rollers," Matthias told him.

Looking up at the second story of the house, which was a good couple of metres above our heads, I asked, "Anybody got a hovercraft?"

"Ha," Matthias chuckled, but then shook his head. "I guess this has been a wasted trip for you dudes."

"Nope, we'll figure it out," I replied, determined to do something to help him and his family. "What gardening gear does your Mum have?"

"I'm not sure. We could go and check in the garage."

"Cool, you guys do that. See if there's anything that will help you clear the grass away from the tennis court and swimming pool. I'm going to run down to church and see what I can do about organising more gear for us."

"You're going to run?" Matthias's eyes went wide.

"Yeah, it's not too far. I'll see you when I get back."

"Uh, okay," he said, heading for the double garage around the side of his house.

I started jogging after him so I could duck through to the driveway, but Ty stopped me with a hand on my wrist.

"You're not doing that thing where you ignore me again are you?" he asked, his eyes barely visible beneath lowered lashes.

"No. I'm just thinking."

"What exactly are you thinking?" he asked.

"Did you even love her?"

Ty scuffed the toe of his *Adidas* sneaker on the concrete path, avoiding my gaze.

"Well?" I asked.

"I cared about her a lot." He shrugged, still not meeting my eyes. "I was never head over heels for her though, and I'm sorry if that hurts you," he finally looked at me, "but I don't want there to be any lies between us. They just ruin everything. Speaking of, is there anything you want to tell me about why you really disappeared from the world for two months?"

"Nope." I shook my head. *Why did he keep asking about that?* "I'm good. And I really should get going. Mattie's counting on me."

"Fine," he sighed, and I took off at a sprint before he hooked me into conversation again.

I had some figuring out to do. I no longer knew what the next right step was, or how best to honour Skye's memory when Ty had ended up with her by accident. It was hard to imagine anyone loving me, but I would rather be alone than in a relationship where I wasn't truly loved. It was easy to imagine someone loving

Skye, and yet Ty hadn't loved her. I didn't know what to make of that.

I hurt for Skye, and yet I hoped for me.

Then I set it all aside while I thought about what gear Matthias needed.

10 minutes later, I jogged around the corner into my church driveway. I slowed down to a walk and headed for my pastor's office, hoping he was there. I wasn't sure what his work hours were. As luck would have it, Pastor Bailor was just unlocking the church when I arrived.

"Hello, Nova." He looked at me with eyes that never stopped twinkling behind his rectangular glasses. "What a lovely surprise. We've missed you at church lately. To what do I owe the honour today?"

His statement made me feel a little bit guilty about avoiding church, but I knew he meant well so I ignored that. I had been thinking about what I would say to him as I ran and had my speech already prepared. I launched into it right there outside the church entrance: "There's a family in our community that's really struggling right now."

"Oh, that's not good," Pastor Bailor said, and I could tell his response was genuine.

"Yeah," I agreed. "They're the Smith family. I'm friends with their son, Matthias, through school. Mrs Smith is having a flare up of *MS*, which has her bedridden, and Mr Smith is trying to hold things together, but I've heard his business isn't doing so well. They're having a hard time making ends meet. They want to sell their house and downsize to take some of the financial pressure off, but don't have the time or money to put into getting their house market-worthy. With all the problems they've been having, they haven't been able to take care of their property, and it needs some serious work. I wondered if there was something our church could do to help them out. A couple of my friends and I have volunteered to do whatever work is needed, but the problem is that we don't have any gear to actually do it with."

"I see." Pastor Bailor nodded with a compassionate expression on his narrow upturned face. "I think it's wonderful that you're willing to help this family. That's exactly what the body of Christ is called to do, and it thrills me to see you putting that into action. What sort of equipment do you think you'll need?"

"The main thing is scaffolding. We need to paint the top story of their house, but can't even reach it with a ladder. A water-blaster would also come in handy. And… I don't know how possible this is, but my ultimate dream would be to build them a patio and do a bit of landscaping, since their yard is basically an overgrown grass jungle."

"Well, I think we can help with some of that at least. The Richmond family has scaffolding they're happy to lend out to other church families, so I'll give them a call to organise that for you. You're also very welcome to borrow my water-blaster, and I'll have a talk to Louise about the patio and landscaping to see if she has any ideas about how we can achieve that dream for the Smiths."

"Thank you so much!" I clapped my hands together. "This will mean so much to them. You have no idea."

"Would you like the water-blaster now?" Pastor Bailor asked, smiling warmly at me.

"Yes, please!"

He rang his wife, Louise, asking her to dig the water-blaster out of the garage for me.

"Louise will bring it around soon," he told me after ending the call. "I've got some work to do inside, but Louise can take you wherever you need to go when she gets here."

I thanked him and then said, "By the way, I'm planning to come back to church this Sunday. I just had some stuff I needed to work through with God."

Pastor Bailor smiled and said, "I'm very glad to hear that, Nova. God is big enough to handle anything you have to throw at him, so never be afraid to ask the tough questions. He has the answers."

Thanking him, I went to sit on a tyre swing in the church playground while I waited for Mrs Bailor. She drove into the car park about 15 minutes later in her red station wagon.

Rolling down her car window, she called out, "Morning, Nova. How lovely to see you! Jump in."

I climbed into the passenger seat and gave Mrs Bailor directions to Matthias's house. On the way, I gave her the same spiel I'd given Pastor Bailor about the Smith family.

"This is the place?" she asked, tucking her dark-brown hair behind her ears so she could eye up the Smiths' house after we had parked on the street outside.

"Yup," I said, jumping out to unload the water-blaster from her car boot.

"I see what you mean about it needing work," she leaned her head out of her window to say to me. "But it's a big place with good bones. If we can help them get it tidied up, it should sell for quite a bit."

"I hope so," I said, carrying the water-blaster around to the driver's side window to carry on my conversation with her. "I guess all we can do is try. Thank you again for your help."

"You're very welcome, Nova. I'll have a think about what else we can do to help them. Do you think they'd appreciate some meals? Our church has a stock of them in the freezer that we've made to give to people in the community. Usually mums with new bubs, but we also try to help people whenever illness strikes."

"I'm sure the Smiths would appreciate that," I said, struck by her thoughtfulness and willingness to help me, especially since I hadn't been to church since Skye had died.

"Okay." Mrs Bailor nodded. "I'll drop some meals around

later today."

I thanked her and lugged the water-blaster around to the back of the house, where I found Ty, Matthias, and Peter ripping Kikuyu out from where it had trailed onto the tennis court. It still looked like a mess out there, but I could already see how much better it would be when they were done.

"Check out what I got," I called, holding up the nozzle of the water-blaster.

"Hey, that's awesome," Ty yelled back. "We'll be able to water-blast the court after we're done here. It should come up real nice."

"Yeah, and the pool and the house too," I said.

"Score, Nova." Matthias dumped a handful of grass into a wheelbarrow and wiped his sweaty forehead with his forearm. "Where did you get it from?"

"My pastor leant it to me. He's pretty sure he'll be able to hook us up with scaffolding too, so we can paint the top story of your house. I'm going to go set this up and clean whatever I can reach."

"You are a blimmen legend, Nova Samson." Matthias grinned at me.

I grinned back and then went to find a hose to connect the water-blaster to, feeling like I was finally doing something right with my life.

CHAPTER
Twenty-Nine

After three days of seriously hard slog – weeding and water-blasting – the backyard looked brand new. My hands had turned to jelly after holding the vibrating water-blaster for hours on end, but it gave me such a rush to see the dirt and lichen strip away from the bricks and concrete that I kept at it anyway.

When Sunday arrived, I'd never felt so grateful to have a day of rest. I bet the Israelites felt a similar relief after 400 years of slavery, when God kindly wrote it in stone that they *had* to take a day off each week. Funnily enough, Pastor Bailor's sermon was based on Exodus that morning, and I was there to take notes.

Mid-morning on Monday, Matthias texted to say the scaffolding had shown up. We converged on his backyard and spent a frustrating hour trying to set it up.

Tempers flared until Peter took charge. "Nobody is allowed to touch anything until I say so," he commanded. He spent several minutes examining all the pieces and moving them into piles before telling us exactly what to grab and where to slot it. With his guidance, it came together in under an hour.

"That was *uh-mayz*ing," I told him when the scaffolding was assembled. "What I wouldn't give to spend a day inside that brain of yours."

"It is pretty epic in here," he grinned, rubbing a hand through his spiky hair, "but overwhelming to mere mortals."

The scaffolding was tall enough for us to reach the roofline, but only long enough to reach half the length of the house at a time. I hauled the water-blaster up with me and hosed all the peeling paint off that I could reach. It came off way too easily, showing how long it had been since the house was painted.

Then we all climbed up on the scaffolding together and worked from opposite ends of it in pairs, painting. I cut in for Ty with a paintbrush while he rolled on the primer with an extendable roller. We mostly worked in silence, apart from the occasional instruction or request for help in certain spots. Matthias cut in for Peter at their end of the scaffolding, but they were making a lot more noise, singing terribly while they painted.

I hated that this distance had crept back in between me and Ty ever since our conversation at Kitekite Falls. I wanted things to go back to normal.

Putting my hand on his wrist to stop him painting for a moment, I said, "Thank you for being honest with me about how you and Skye got together."

"No worries," he said, looking down at me with warmth and affection. "Still friends?"

"Always." I nodded seriously before cracking a grin. "You could have fake dated one of my sisters and I'd still be your friend."

He chuckled, but said, "We weren't fake dating. It was real. I just wouldn't have chosen it under different circumstances."

What different circumstances? I wondered, but didn't ask.

After a while, Ty began singing along to the Ed Sheeran song that was playing on Matthias's speaker. I listened in awe. His voice was so rich and gorgeous.

"Have you written any more songs since the one you sang at Skye's funeral?" I asked him, dipping my brush into the paint bucket for what felt like the hundredth time that day.

"Nothing worth listening to." He chuckled ruefully.

"That's a shame," I said sincerely. "The song you wrote for Skye was beautiful."

"Thanks," he said, but shook his head.

After a moment, he began singing again, and I joined in with the alto harmony. Ty grinned when he heard me and held his paint roller in front of my mouth like a microphone. I did the same for him, crossing arms with him to hold my paint brush in front of his mouth. His eyes sparkled into mine as we belted out the chorus to *Perfect*.

Peter and Matthias started hooting and clapping from their end of the scaffolding, so we bowed for them when we finished the song and then smiled fondly at each other before resuming our painting. Joy bubbled up inside of me as Ty and I continued to sing and work together for the rest of the day. Simply being in his presence made me so happy, even doing something as mundane as painting a house.

With all four of us up on the scaffolding, we made fast work of that first section of the house. By the end of the day, we had already completed a coat of primer and two coats of the sandy-coloured top coat.

Matthias's dad came out to thank us after he got back from work that evening and said he was going to get the pool running so we could cool off on our breaks. That sounded like seven kinds of deliciousness. Until then, I had to settle for a lukewarm shower at home to cool down instead.

On Tuesday, we unlocked the wheels and unhooked the braces on the scaffolding so that we could roll it along the grass to the other half of the rear wall, where we secured it again and repeated the cleaning and painting process. Mr Smith had filled the pool overnight, so it now taunted us with its sparkling blue water while we painted in the hot sun. That summer was a muggy one, and my face glistened no matter how many times I wiped it.

At midday, we stopped to let the primer coat dry. After washing the paint off our hands as best we could and eating *Marmite* and cheese sandwiches in the Smiths' work-worn kitchen, all four of us jumped into the pool. The boys had worn board shorts to paint in so they would be ready to swim. I had been wearing togs under my painting clothes, so I stripped down to those. The pool was only heated by the sun and, since it hadn't even sat under a day's worth of sunshine yet, it was frigidly cold. That didn't bother me though. I was so hot and itchy from painting that I relished every cool caress on my body.

I was a starfish on top of the water when somebody launched into me from underneath and threw me up into the air. I landed with a splash on my butt in the water and whipped around to see who had thrown me. All the boys were laughing, so I couldn't tell who the culprit was. Since Matthias was usually the prankster of our group, I decided to jump on his back and push him under. I threw myself at him, but he was so big and solid that he didn't even budge. He just grabbed my legs and flipped me backwards off him. I landed upside-down in the water again.

"You are so dead!" I half-yelled, half-laughed when I resurfaced.

"You really think itty-bitty little you can take on big hulking me?" he faux sneered, beating his chest like a Viking warrior. "In your dreams, Nova Scotia."

Nova Scotia was Mattie's nickname for me. Everyone seemed to have one. Apparently, Nova was just one of those names people liked to play around with.

Ty gestured at me over Matthias's shoulder, doing some complicated hand signals I didn't fully understand. I at least figured out enough to know he wanted us to gang up on Matthias, so I rushed at Matthias again to distract him while Ty dove under the water and went for his legs. I launched myself onto Mattie's shoulders at the same moment Ty pulled his legs out from under him. Matthias fell backwards as I leapt away. He came up roaring, shaking water from his thick brown hair as he yelled, "That's it. You're both going down. You with me Liu?"

"Hell yeah!" Peter yelled.

It was war. We spent a good hour fighting, team against team, and I got dunked and thrown up into the air far more than my fair share. On a racetrack I could have whipped both Peter and Matthias, but in the pool their heavier boy-muscles gave them an unfair advantage. Ty protected me as much as he could, throwing his body in front of mine whenever the guys came at me, and then eventually lifting me onto his shoulders so that he could keep me out of their reach.

I fell a little bit more in love with him for that.

Finally, we dragged ourselves laughing out of the pool to get back to the business of painting the Smiths' house. The boys just stayed in their wet board shorts, bare chested. I slipped my clothes back on over my dripping togs and tried not to look at Ty, who had the nicest body of all the guys – tall and sculpted, like he'd been chiselled out of warm stone. My cutting-in got a lot sloppier when he stretched up to roll paint on the wall, and all the muscles in his back rippled in concert. I forgot to paint all together when he took a drink from his water bottle and then licked a drop of water from his pouty bottom lip.

He noticed me watching him and cocked the bottle towards me. "You thirsty?"

"So thirsty," I said, taking the proffered bottle and placing my lips where his had just been.

Ty watched me as I drank, biting down on his lip the entire time. I felt myself flush as I imagined meeting his lips with my own.

If only.

I handed the bottle back to him and we carried on painting, but there was a new palpable tension between us. I hadn't felt anything like it since that moment when he watched me jump into the waterhole at Kitekite Falls.

It must have got Ty wondering again about the things I hadn't told him, because he used the semi-privacy we had down our end of the scaffolding to say, "Since I've been so open and honest with you lately, I think it's only fair that you return the favour. Are you ever going to tell me why you shut me out after Skye's funeral?"

He wasn't going to give up. He was like a seagull eying up a cup of hot chips. Nothing was going to distract him from feasting on my secret. I stopped my cutting-in for a minute to watch him roll paint while I decided how best to respond. A baseball cap covered his hair, but it somehow only served to highlight his slanted cheekbones, straight nose, and angular jaw. I loved his lips best of all though. A couple of his bottom teeth were twisted at a 45-degree angle, and they pushed his bottom lip out in a permanent pout. That pout had featured in many of my most vivid daydreams over the past year. I'd never kissed a boy before, but I sure as heck had dreamed about kissing Ty.

What if I did tell him about my feelings for him? What would happen? He might say, "Hallelujah! Finally! I feel the exact same way." And then we would get together and potentially live happily ever after.

Or he might say, "Well, this is awkward, but I've never thought of you like that." And then everything between us would be ruined, and I would have to hide away in embarrassment, lonely and alone once again, with no one to talk to since Matthias and Peter were more Ty's friends than mine.

Or, what if I told him I liked him, and he was too nice to tell me he wasn't interested? We could end up falling into a relationship he didn't even want, like he'd done with Skye.

Yeah, there was definitely no way I could be honest with him about this.

"Some things are better off not shared." I settled on my

answer.

"But most things are better off when they are," he retorted.

"Whatever it is, Nova, you can trust me with it."

"Maybe I'll tell you one day, when it doesn't hurt so much."
That was nicely vague and mysterious.

He shook his head like he disagreed, but didn't argue any further.

After that, we carried on painting and occasionally singing along to the music Matthias was playing, but it felt like we had lost the warm camaraderie between us.

CHAPTER

Thirty

On Wednesday, I could immediately tell something was off with Ty. He refused to meet my eye. In fact, he seemed to have adopted all the same tricks I had used in my two-month hiatus from life. It caused a heavy weight to settle in my stomach. I wanted to wave my hands in front of his face and demand he look at me, but that didn't seem fair.

My suspicions only grew when Matthias bowled up to me and said, "You're with me today, Nova Scotia. Pete wants to talk nerd stuff with Ty. Us cool cats are sticking together."

He was trying to act like everything was normal, but I knew it wasn't. The compulsive wringing of his hands on the bottom of his red t-shirt was a dead giveaway, as was the fact his face had taken on a glow to match his tee.

But I was in no place to kick up a fuss, so I just replied, "Cool," and then shouted a little louder so that Ty and Peter could hear me, "Let's get to work, children."

Despite everything, working with Matthias was fun. Although I did end up covered in a lot more paint than I had on either of the previous days. He flicked it at me whenever I said anything annoying, and he wiped his paint-covered hands on my back, claiming he'd lost his clean-up cloth somewhere. I told him repeatedly he could use my rag, but he just smirked at me.

And then, somewhere in hour two, his face took on a serious expression as he placed his roller in the paint tray, stood up, and said, "So, what's the dealio with you and Ty?"

"What do you mean?" I asked, scrunching my forehead like I didn't know exactly what he meant.

"You guys have been friends forever, and it's always been a comfortable sort of arrangement, like whānau. But lately I could slice the air around you with a spatula. You're hot. You're cold. You're sleeping in his bed, then you're not speaking to him for months. You're back to living in each other's pockets and outdoing each other on who can be the most perfect specimen, except something is up. There's a tension in the air that never used to be there. So, I ask you again, what's the dealio?"

Wow. Mattie was a lot more observant than I'd ever given him credit for. Which sucked for me. Now there was one more person I had to try and keep my secret from.

Unless... I didn't.

Could I confide in Matthias? Could I trust him to keep my secret? There wasn't anyone else I could tell. I had been holding it in for more than a year, but in that time the secret had become a vice holding me.

"Can I trust you with something?" I asked him.

His eyes flared with excitement, but he just nodded and said, "Of course."

"No, I mean, can I really trust you? If I tell you this, you can't go and tell Peter. You can't tell your cat, or your mum, or your surfboard. If I confide in you, I am the only person you can talk to about this. Do you promise?"

"I promise," Matthias rumbled in his deep voice and held up a little finger to pinkie swear with me.

"Okay. Cool. Cool. Cool. Cool," I nervously mimicked Jake Peralta from *Brooklyn 99* as I locked pinkies with Mattie. Although part of me *was* nervous, another part of me felt lighter at the prospect of sharing this burden with him. I didn't have to carry it alone anymore. And then the words just fell out of me: "I realised I was in love with Ty about one hour before he got together with Skye."

Mattie's small grey eyes widened. Significantly.

"The last year has been absolute torture for me," I continued. "And now, Skye's gone, and I don't know how to act around Ty anymore. I know he needs me to be his friend, but that's so hard when I have all these feelings for him getting in the way."

Mattie's face was doing a strange thing – breaking into an enormous contorted grin as he wheeze-laughed and bent over, slapping his hefty thighs.

"Are you okay?" I asked him.

"So okay." He laughed. "I totally called this. I *knew* you were into him. Oh man, this is going to be a hell of a secret to keep from everyone. You sure I can't tell Liu?"

"Oh my gosh, Mattie. No! You promised me." I was wringing *my* hands now.

Matthias chuckled. "Just kidding, Nova. I'll keep your damn secret."

"Thanks," I muttered, halfway reassured.

"So, what are you going to do about it?" he asked me, scooping his roller back up and dragging it back and forth on the grooved part of the paint tray.

"What do you mean?" I frowned, angling my paintbrush to cut in around a window.

"I mean, are you going to tell Ty how you feel?" he asked. "Give him a chance to reciprocate."

"No way! I couldn't do that. Skye's only been gone a couple of months. It wouldn't be right."

"I wouldn't judge you." Matthias shrugged. "I know Pete wouldn't either. Maybe you'd be the best thing for Ty right now."

"I don't want the memory of Skye coming between us," I said

as I dipped my paint brush back into the bucket. "If Ty and I ever do get together, I want it to be because he's as into me as I am into him."

"Fair 'nuff," Matthias said, then added, "but I'm rooting for you."

CHAPTER
Thirty-One

By Saturday, we had worked our way around the entire house and were painting the final wall. Matthias and I had stayed partnered up for the rest of the week, much to my disappointment. I missed Ty, especially since he was still avoiding eye contact with me.

All the days of painting had started to roll together, and I was dreaming about cutting-in at night, but I was so proud of everything we had accomplished.

As soon as we had finished painting the final coat on the last wall and dismantled the scaffolding, Matthias brought his mum outside to show her what we had done. Mrs Smith was a tall woman, like her son, but where he was broad and filled out, she was all bones and knobbly joints. She had the same grey eyes as Matthias, but they appeared much larger in her thin face as she gazed around at the immaculate pool and tennis court. She took in the freshly painted house with an occasional gasp, and it finally dawned on me that she was crying. I teared up a little too, seeing how much our help meant to her.

After she had thanked us all profusely for our work, Matthias helped her back into the house. While he did that, I called Pastor Bailor and told him we were finished with the scaffolding and ready to move onto landscaping, if he had any ideas for how we could accomplish that.

He did have some ideas.

"Louise suggested we put a notice on the community page," he said, "so I did, and got an incredible response from a local landscaping company that has excess tile it's willing to donate. There should be enough to make an eight-by-eight metre patio. The company is even willing to donate the rest of the materials you'll need to lay it, so all you'll have to do is supply the labour. Are you up for the challenge?"

"We sure are," I said. "Thank you for organising this!"

"You're very welcome, Nova. I'll make sure the patio materials are delivered to the Smiths' house ASAP," Pastor Bailor promised.

"Thank you so much. I can't believe this is really happening."

After ending the call, I told the guys the good news.

We were all smiling and clapping each other on the back until Ty asked, "Anybody know how to lay a patio?"

I shook my head. So did Matthias and Peter.

"Okay," Ty said. "Watch as many *YouTube* tutorials as you can before Monday and we'll coordinate a plan then. Also, scrounge around your houses for any tools that might come in handy. Ones that you see in the tutorials."

"Aye aye, captain." Peter saluted Ty and then asked, "Do you guys want me to give you a lift home?"

"Yeah, thanks," I said.

As soon as Peter had dropped me and Ty off in Ty's driveway and driven off, Ty turned towards his house and walked away from me. He didn't even say goodbye. I hated this. I hated being ignored by him. It was a thousand times worse than when I had stayed away from him because I felt so rejected. I had done this. I had caused this rift between us with my decision to stay away from him and then my decision to never explain why. I needed to fix it, whatever it took.

"Wait," I called after him.

As slowly as a bug caught in a web, Ty rotated to face me.

"What?" he asked, expressionless, but he did take a step closer.

"Do you want to come over and watch patio tutorials with me?" I asked with a casual shrug of my shoulder, masking how terrified I was that he would turn me down. "I can make us popcorn."

"Fine," he replied, and I glimpsed the slightest crack in his façade.

I smiled at him, relieved. "Give me a minute to shower and change out of my stinky painting clothes before you come over, kay?"

Ty stepped closer again and inhaled. "You smell good to me, Nova, but shower if you must."

Oxygen surged through my veins, hauling all the blood to my face, but I decided to be bold and say, "I'd skip it if I smelled as good as you."

Ty's eyes widened, but my courage was spent, so I lifted my hand in farewell and darted across the street to the safety of my house.

By the time I had showered and scrubbed as much of the paint off me as I could find, I was composed again. Unfortunately, choosing something to wear sent me climbing the walls again. I talked myself down by reminding myself that this was *Ty*. He knew me intimately. I mean, not *intimately*, but *well*. He already knew what I looked like; what clothes I owned. He knew I preferred clothes that let me move freely. He knew me the way I knew him. And I loved him, effortlessly. I wanted him to fall for the real me if he was going to, so I wore the clothes that made me feel good – a simple combination of shorts and t-shirt that left me ready for anything.

By the time Ty arrived at my house, he was also freshly showered; his damp hair tousled and his skin smelling of soap.

He'd changed into shorts and a t-shirt too, but he looked way better in them than I did, with his darker skin and hard muscles. I swallowed around the painful lump in my throat that his untouchable presence always caused me. Ty seemed blithely unaffected by my presence. He just smiled a somewhat reserved, crooked smile and said, "Where are we watching?"

"My room." I nodded towards the stairs. "Head on up, and I'll bring the popcorn.

"Right then." He nodded and wandered up my creaky staircase.

I bustled into the kitchen to get the popcorn cooking in butter on the stove. When it was done popping, I poured it into a big ceramic bowl and ground salt over the top before placing it on a tray. I added a couple of glasses of Mum's homemade lemonade to the tray and carried the whole lot up to my bedroom.

Ty was there, sitting on my bed and leaning against my tufted headboard. I had the urge to drop the tray and throw myself into his arms. Instead, I sedately placed the tray on his lap and went to close my Roman blinds so we would have darkness for our tutorial watching. I flicked on my bedside lamp to give the room a cosy low-lit feel and then hopped onto the bed next to Ty, pulling my computer onto my lap.

I could smell Ty's shampoo as I opened YouTube and searched for DIY patio tutorials. He was stiff beside me. He hadn't even eaten any of the popcorn yet.

"This laptop is going to burn my legs if I don't get under the duvet," I said by way of explanation as I climbed properly into my bed and pulled the white duvet over my lap. "Feel free to climb in too."

He didn't move for at least 30 seconds, like he was having some sort of internal debate with himself, but finally he pulled the cover down and then back up over his legs. Then he said, "Mum wondered if you wanted to come over to our house for dinner later. She's making stir-fry."

"Thanks, I'd love that. I'll just let my mum know so she doesn't cook for me." I pulled my phone out of my shorts pocket and fired off a quick text to Mum, too lazy to get back out of bed and tell her. Mum replied that she and Dad would have a date night later, since I wouldn't be home. Perfect.

"Alright, good." Ty finally took a small handful of popcorn from the bowl as I clicked on the most promising-looking tutorial on *YouTube*.

"Here we go," I said.

We watched three tutorials in a row, sitting side by side in my bed. I was so conscious of Ty's presence that I had to focus extra hard to take in anything about laying patios.

"Lots of tools involved," Ty commented as I finally shut my laptop.

"Yeah, levels and string-lines and stuff I didn't even know existed. Let's go ask my dad if he's got any of it before he leaves with Mum."

"Sounds good. I'll just write a list so we don't forget anything." Ty found a scrap of paper on my desk and jotted down what tools we'd need, with me pitching in ideas when he forgot something. Then we found my dad in the lounge and asked him for help. He took us down to the garage where he was able to dig up most of what we needed. We texted our list to Peter and Matthias, telling them what tools we had and asking if they could source the rest. I was a little nervous about how it would all come together on Monday, but hoped we'd be able to make the patio look decent.

At around 6pm, Ty and I headed across the road to his house for dinner, which was such a flavourful and delicious chicken stir-fry, I ate seconds. My weight had started to creep back up again in the past couple of weeks, and I was looking more like myself. Not so gaunt.

After eating dinner with Ty and his parents, I began making

moves towards the front door. I figured I'd probably inflicted enough of myself on Ty for one evening, but he grabbed my hand and asked, "You want to stay a bit longer? We could watch an actual movie."

"Sure." I nodded, as his hand burned a glorious spike of hot longing up my arm.

"Sweet." His head dropped forward so his hair covered his eyes, but I could still see his mouth where he'd tucked his bottom lip in between his teeth. Obviously, something about me staying mattered to him. I didn't know what was going on in his head. All I knew was that I'd hated him ignoring me this past week and would do anything to make him smile again. I followed him through to his bedroom.

"Here you go." Ty smoothed a beige throw blanket over my legs. Then he jumped onto the bed next to me, fluffed up a pillow behind him, and yanked the blanket his way to cover his legs too.

That pulled it off one of my legs so I yelled, "Oi, blanket hog!" and yanked it back my way.

"There's an easy solution to this problem." Ty scooched closer to me until his hip was almost flush with mine. The back of his hand knocked into mine with the scooch, and it was like all the Whos in Whoville were singing and setting off fireworks on my skin. Even after Ty moved his hand away to click play on the *Marvel* movie we'd chosen, I could still feel where his touch had branded my skin.

Luckily the movie was good, or I would have been too lost in Ty's closeness to get sucked into it. I may have been a little hopped up on nerves anyway because I completely lost it at a slightly funny part of the movie, laughing so hard I doubled over on his bed.

When it was obvious that I wasn't calming down anytime soon, Ty paused the movie and asked, "You a'ight there, Samson?"

I was laughing too hard to answer him. The ridiculous scene

kept replaying in my mind, and I was so giddy about hanging out with Ty like this – almost like a date – that I couldn't calm down.

Ty started laughing at me laughing, which made me laugh even harder. Pretty soon I was gasping for breath.

"Sit tight," Ty said. "I'm going to get you a drink of water before you choke." He left and was gone for so long, I did eventually calm down. When he finally returned, he was carrying a tray with a glass of water, two hot chocolates, and a small cheeseboard spread. "Here you go, Nova Brie." He set the tray down on my lap.

It felt like a date. It really did. To me at least, who had never been on one before. But when the movie had finished, and we'd cleaned up our dishes, all Ty said was, "I guess I'll see you on Patio Monday. Mum's going to drive me to Mattie's. You wanna catch a ride?"

"Yeah, thanks. No sense wasting petrol, what with the current prices."

Great, now I was making awkward small talk like my parents. Petrol prices were something they loved discussing.

And that was that. Ty saw me out, hugged me goodnight, and I was no closer to knowing how he felt about me than I'd ever been. And definitely no closer to knowing why he'd ignored me all week.

Well played, sir. Well played.

CHAPTER

Thirty-Two

"Surprise!" Peter and Matthias yelled when Ty and I rounded the corner into the Smiths' backyard on Monday morning. The patio was already laid.

"What the heck?" My features twisted in astonishment as I stared at the large slab of stone pavers. "How did this happen?"

Peter was so excited, he was hopping from foot to foot like a little kid who needed to pee. "Someone dropped the stuff off on Saturday night after you left, so Mattie thought it would be cool to lay it yesterday and surprise you. His dad helped us."

"It looks mint." Ty crouched down and ran a hand over one of the limestone tiles. "You guys crushed it."

"Yeah, Dad's stoked with how it turned out." Matthias nodded. "I think it was good he did some of the work because, to be honest, I haven't seen him look so chuffed in a long time. He even mowed the lawns afterwards."

"Man, that's so good." I smiled. "Is there anything left for us to do?"

"We just need to get the grout in now that the tiles have set, and then dig and plant the gardens on either side of the patio." Matthias pointed to the spots he meant. "Dad's given me some money to go to the garden centre and pick something out, but

I've got no idea what to choose."

None of us had any idea about plants, so we all stood there with bewildered expressions.

"Can we *YouTube* garden ideas?" Ty asked.

"*Pinterest!*" I exclaimed. "We can *Pinterest* them."

"Oh, hell no," Peter said. "*Pinterest* is a black hole that sucks you in and doesn't even spit out your desiccated remains."

"And you would know that how?" Matthias raised a curious eyebrow at Peter.

"Robotics, man." Peter nodded like that explained anything at all.

We were all staring blankly at him, so he pulled out his phone, which I noted had the *Pinterest* app on the front page. Peter clicked into it and held it up to show us a board pinned with robotics images and tutorials.

"So, this is what you're doing when you're not answering your texts." Ty slow-nodded like so many things suddenly made sense.

"Yeah." Peter's grin was sheepish. "This is what I would've been doing for the past couple of weeks if you punks hadn't roped me into this. I'm pretty keen to be done with the backyard reno if I'm honest, even though it's been cool and all."

"Let's kick this out then," I said. "Bring up New Zealand landscaping ideas, Pete. I'll make a plant list while you guys finish the grout and dig the gardens. Then you can drive us all to the garden centre to buy the plants and whatever else we need. Sound good?"

"Sounds friggin' amazing." Peter smiled.

Three hours later, I was bedding in the last of the sun-hungry plants we'd chosen while the boys cleaned up the tools and swept the new patio.

"Let's post this so we can thank the landscaping company," I said.

I snapped a photo of the new patio and gardens and then rounded up the boys for a shot with all of us in it. Ty wrapped his arm around me from the left, and Matthias wrapped his arm around me from the right. Peter was on the end, so he connected my phone to a selfie stick and held it up to photograph us all standing on the new patio.

"Cool. I'll post this and then we are officially *done*," I proclaimed.

"Hell yes!!!" Peter yelled. "About time. Last one in the pool's a rotten egg."

He took off at a run, Ty right behind him. I was looking for somewhere to stash my phone when Matthias cleared his throat and said, "Hey, Nova. On a scale of one to ten, how mad would you be if Pete guessed you like Ty?"

"Hulk smash mad. Why?" I asked him.

"Oh, no reason." He took off sprinting towards the pool, cannonballing in and sending water surging over the side.

Well, that wasn't suspicious at all. Man, I was a fool for telling Matthias. I should have known he wouldn't be able to keep it a secret, pinkie-promise or not. Well, nothing I could do about it now.

I'd taken to wearing my black padded bikini under my clothes since we were always swimming on our breaks, so I stripped off my shorts and t-shirt, deposited them on top of my phone, and then ran and dived into the pool too.

When I came up for air, Ty startled me by looming in front of me. "Mattie's acting suss. What did he say to you?"

"Uh…" I turned to look at Matthias and Peter, who were watching me and Ty with obvious glee on both their faces. "He was just apologising for being a *sucky* friend." I really emphasised "sucky" for Matthias's benefit. He had the grace to look ashamed.

Ty glanced at Matthias and then back at me and said, "Okay. Cool. Cool. Cool. Cool. Cool. Cool. Cool."

Great, now he was nervously imitating Jake Paralta.

"What did you think he was talking to me about?" I asked.

"No, nothing. Nothing."

That second "nothing" convinced me it wasn't nothing at all, but Ty back-flipped away from me, effectively ending our conversation.

We all splashed and played in the pool for a good hour before Peter drove me and Ty back home, and we parted ways.

As I walked up the brick path to my front door, I realised Ty was becoming a mystery I wanted to solve, but I had no idea how to go about it.

CHAPTER
Thirty-Three

An epic Samson family Christmas was exactly the kind of distraction I needed. I had been spending so much time with the guys lately that I was looking forward to my sisters' overt femaleness.

Mum organised it so that my sisters, brother-in-law, niece, and nephew all spent the night at our house on Christmas Eve. She was super excited about Paton hanging up her Christmas stocking over our fireplace for the first time. She had even hand-sewn her a pink stocking with a fluffy angel on its front. Our stone fireplace was getting awfully crowded, what with nine Christmas stockings arranged above it this year.

We ate a simple chicken curry together on the night before Christmas, saving room for the next day's feast. Then we sat around the living room, singing Christmas carols accompanied by Gretchen on the piano. Arlo made us laugh with his vigorous dance moves on the centre rug, which mostly included a lot of hopping and spinning. Paton had only just started walking, so she got her groove on by bouncing steadily on the spot.

"She gets her dance moves from me," Mark joked.

"You wish you were that good a dancer," Veronica ribbed him.

"Thanks for that, wife," Mark deadpanned, and we all

laughed.

It was there, cosying up on the couch next to Mum and Dad with the rest of my family around me, I realised I had so much to be thankful for. I had just lost sight of it for a while.

Since Melody was always flexing about the free swag she got from her vlog sponsors, Mum gave her the job of filling all the stockings after the rest of us went to bed. I was expecting quite the haul of moisturiser and makeup come Christmas morning. Maybe I'd actually figure out what to do with it one of these days.

A way-too-excited Arlo woke us all up at half-past six on Christmas morning, so I decided to make the most of the early start and go for a run.

Melody was sitting at the breakfast bar, rugged up in a fluffy dressing gown and drinking a cup of coffee when I returned. "I can't believe you went for a run on Christmas morning!" she exclaimed, shaking her head over her mug.

"I love it." I shrugged. Most people thought running was some kind of cruel torture, but it had always made me feel better. "It helps clear my head."

"Why do you feel like you need to clear your head?" she asked me.

"Well, you know… because otherwise life would feel too overwhelming," I tried to explain, waving my hand in a vague gesture.

Melody just looked at me thoughtfully for a minute, and then said, "Have you ever wondered whether running away from your emotions was actually doing you more harm than good?"

"Huh?" I scrunched my forehead.

"Life's really hard." She clonked down her oversized coffee cup as if to emphasise her point. "We're constantly experiencing frustrations, misunderstandings, disappointments, and loss."

"Yeeeeah… I know. I mean, I did just lose my best friend," I said testily.

"I know you did, and I'm so sorry," she replied, reaching out a hand to grasp mine. "I'm not trying to be insensitive, but this is important. Every time your emotions get stirred up, you have a choice to make. Do you process those emotions, or do you try to distract yourself from them? I think you run to distract yourself from what you're feeling, but it's not doing you any favours."

"But it helps me mentally so much," I argued, feeling a little offended by her unsolicited commentary on my life. "And running's good for me. Everybody knows exercise is healthy."

"Exercise in and of itself is healthy," Melody agreed, squeezing my hand before letting it go to pick up her coffee cup again. "But it's not healthy when you use it to flee from your feelings."

"What makes you think that's what I'm doing?" I asked her.

"Because," she said, "I used to go shopping to distract myself from my feelings, and it took a lot of counselling to get me to a place where I could recognise that's what I was doing. Now I can spot the signs. You've probably got away with it for so long because people do think exercise is healthy. If you were overeating, or drinking, or playing too many video games, I'm sure Mum and Dad would have intervened long ago."

"So, what do you think I should do instead?" I asked, feeling like the kitchen tiles under my feet had suddenly tipped sideways. "I don't want to give up running. I love it."

"You don't have to give it up," Melody reassured me, shaking her head briefly. "You just need to make sure you're giving yourself space at some point in your day to really feel your feelings."

"How do I do that?"

"Well, some people journal; others pray. I do both. Sometimes I write poetry when I'm feeling especially overwhelmed. Other times, I run a deep bubble bath and listen to music that matches my emotions, so I can really experience them. The trick is to be intentional about trying to understand what your emotions are telling you. They're there for a reason, but if you keep pushing them down, you'll never come to understand yourself. And if you push them down for too long, you might find your feelings bursting out in anger at the people around you, or you might find that anger turning inwards on yourself in self-loathing and depression. Neither scenario is good."

"Okay," I said. "That sounds scary."

"Yeah, well it can be. That's why I wanted to say something to you – so you can start taking better care of yourself."

"I am taking care of myself," I retorted. "I already feel like I'm doing heaps better than I was when Skye died."

"Well, good." Melody smiled. "I'm glad. Now dig into those feelings and try to work out why you're doing better, and if there are any thoughts or feelings you haven't addressed yet."

"Okay." I nodded, making a move to leave the kitchen. "I'll try."

"Good. But before you go, there is one last thing I should warn you about."

"Mmmm?" I said.

"Just be aware that sometimes your feelings will try to lie to you – tell you things like nobody wants you around, or you're not good enough, or you're not worthy of love."

It was like she could see right inside my brain, and suddenly she had my full attention.

Melody continued: "So I suggest spending time every day reading your Bible, letting it wash you in the truth. Eventually, you should find your thoughts and feelings lining up with God's truth about who you are and who he made you to be."

"Okay. Read my Bible and journal my feelings every day. Got it," I said, and I was being serious. "We're a week early for New Year's resolutions, but maybe I could make some Christmas resolutions this year instead."

"I like that idea." Melody beamed at me. "Maybe I'll do the same."

She stood up and walked around the breakfast bar to my side, where she opened her arms for a hug. I sunk into her fluffy-robed embrace and felt surprisingly glad that I had such a wise older sister looking out for me.

When Melody released me, and I was finally able to go upstairs to shower, I promised myself that I would start reading my Bible and keeping a journal every day. It made me feel hopeful about my life in a new way. I wondered what secrets I had been keeping from myself, and what truths God wanted to reveal to me.

Mum must have heard my feet hit the stairs on my way back down after I had got dressed, because she immediately called the whole family together to follow her outside to the driveway. A near-new *Nissan Leaf* was parked behind Dad's car. It hadn't been there when I went for my run.

"Merry Christmas, Nova!" Mum and Dad bellowed, smiling at me.

"What?" I screeched. "Is that for me?"

"It sure is," Dad confirmed, handing me the car key. "We love you, Nova Brie. We wanted you to have a way to get yourself around."

Everyone was smiling as I took the key from Dad and then launched myself into his arms for a hug. "Thank you so much. This is amazing. I was not expecting it, at all."

"You're welcome." He hugged me back. "The best part is that you can charge it right here at home, so it won't cost you much to run."

"Well, while I appreciate being able to charge it here for free, I think that the best part is actually the car." I laughed. "Can I take it for a spin?"

"Go for gold," Dad told me.

I spent a couple of minutes enjoying the smooth glide of my new car as I drove it up and down our road, but then parked it back in the driveway and went inside because I knew Mum would want my help in the kitchen.

Sure enough, as soon as I walked through the front door, she roped me into being her sous-chef. We always ate our largest meal at lunchtime on Christmas day, which made for a busy morning of chopping herbs, peeling root vegetables, whipping cream, and topping beans, all while the intoxicating smell of roasting chicken and lamb drifted out of the oven, and caused our stomachs to howl in mutiny.

"I need you to set both the dining table and the outdoor table," Mum instructed, opening the cutlery drawer for me.

"Why both?" I asked, grabbing a handful of knives and forks. "We've got enough seats inside." Our farmhouse table seated 10.

"Because I've invited the Tyler family to join us today," she explained, turning her back on me to whisk the cheese sauce that had started bubbling on the stovetop. "With the year they've had, it was the least I could do."

"Okay." I nodded, and my heart didn't know whether to hammer with nerves or excitement. I'd have to journal about that later.

CHAPTER
Thirty-Four

The front doorbell rang in the middle of Gretchen telling Melody, Veronica, and me all about her new boyfriend, Dan. We weren't able to meet him this Christmas because his parents lived in the South Island, so he was spending the holidays down there. I could tell that Gretchen was really into him though, so I was sure we would meet him soon enough.

"Nova, can you get that?" Mum asked me as she skewered one of the roast chickens with a meat thermometer. "I'm a little busy here."

"Sure thing," I attempted to sound normal, even though the doorbell had my insides crawling their way to my outsides. I had only been away from Ty for a few days, but was already on edge about seeing him again. There was still so much unknown between us.

I opened the door to a dressed-up Rosamie Tyler holding a large salad, and a tie-wearing James Tyler carrying a pavlova slathered in whipped cream and strawberries. Their two children stood behind them, Ty wearing a closely fitted navy shirt and sleek pair of trousers, while his older (but much shorter) sister, Alex, had also dressed up for the occasion in a pleated ruby dress and matching *Wizard-of-Oz*-worthy shoes.

"Merry Christmas!" they all exclaimed.

"Merry Christmas!" I replied, grinning.

"I'll go and pop this in the kitchen." Rosamie winked as she drifted past me to the room where she'd spent many hours preserving fruit and making lemon curd with my mother over the years. James followed her with the pavlova and a nod in my direction.

Ty held a silver-wrapped gift box in his hands, but Alex was empty-handed, so I opened my arms out wide to give her a hug. I hadn't seen her since Skye's funeral. She must have just arrived home from Dunedin for Christmas.

"When did you get back?" I asked Alex, leading her and Ty around the corner and into the living room.

"Just a couple of days ago," she replied, taking a seat on one of our blue velvet armchairs. Ty sat down on the other one, resting the silver present on his knees. "I was road-tripping around the South Island with uni friends until last week."

"Mint. Where'd you go?" I asked her, sitting down on our couch.

"Most of the deep South and the West Coast," she said, her hazel eyes taking on a dreamy look. "Milford Sound was stunning, but it took forever to get to. Worth it though. Even the drive there was mind-blowing. I think it's the most beautiful place I've ever seen."

"I've never even been to the South Island." I scrunched my nose. Mum and Dad had taken my older sisters on a big South Island road trip several years before I was born and never repeated the experience. "Am I missing much?"

"Come visit me in Dunedin and find out. You'd be welcome to crash on my couch anytime. You too, little brother." She turned to Ty to include him in our conversation.

"Sounds like a plan," he said. "Maybe Nova and I could road trip down when I get my driver confidence back. If that ever happens." Ty shrugged ruefully and then inclined his head towards me. "What d'ya reckon? Would you be game for an adventure?"

"Definitely." I smiled, thrilled by the thought of all those hours cosied up with him in a car. "You'd better get driving again soon then, because I'm going to hold you to this."

"Deal." He grinned, looking as excited as I felt. "I can't imagine anything better than a road trip with you, my guitar, and maybe our surfboards."

"Me neither." I beamed at him.

Alex watched this whole exchange with a bemused expression, before I distracted her with questions about university life. Outwardly I appeared calm, but inwardly I was buzzing. Ty wanted to spend time alone with me.

After a few minutes more of conversation, Dad called us through to the dining room to eat. The table could barely fit all the food it was serving – two large chickens, one leg of lamb, about six different kinds of roast vegetables, several salads, green beans, broccoli, gravy, and cheese sauce. It smelled like happiness.

When we were all squished together in the narrow dining room that had been built several generations ago, Dad said grace: "Heavenly Father, we thank you for this yearly reminder of how much you love us. Everything we have now and hope to have in the future is because of your love. We thank you for these precious moments today with friends and family. May you bless this food to our bodies and bless our time together. Amen."

"Amen," we all echoed.

"Alright, folks," Dad unclasped his hands and gestured towards the lavish feast we were about to consume, "we won't all fit around the table today, but please fill your plates and find a seat wherever you can, either here in the dining room or outside on the deck. Enjoy!"

"Thank you. Everything looks so delicious." Rosamie smiled as she stepped forward to take a plate. "How can I possibly choose?"

It was a problem we all faced. I hung back while Ty gave it his best shot. He managed to fill his plate to overflowing before he'd even made it a third of the way around the table. I watched him longingly eye up the food he'd missed.

In the back corner of the dining room, I spotted Veronica and Mark clipping silicone catch-all bibs onto Arlo and Paton, who'd been restrained in plastic high chairs. Veronica and Mark set pre-diced selections of Christmas lunch on each high chair tray, so I made my way over to my sister and her husband and said, "If you want, I can watch these two while you get your food."

"That'd be great. Thanks Nova." Mark grinned. "Ronnie's always so busy feeding the munchkins, she forgets to feed herself."

"I think forgetting to eat is the family curse." I smiled at him as Veronica kissed me on the side of my head and went to get her food.

Ty came up beside me then, his plate piled high, and asked, "You want to eat outside with me?"

"I will soon." I nodded towards my niece and nephew. "I'm just watching the cuties while Veronica and Mark eat."

"Here." He thrust his plate into my hand and pulled up a chair for me. "Eat this. I'll go get another plate for me."

"Wow." I laughed, looking down at the plate laden with more potatoes than I'd normally eat in a year. "Thanks, but this is way too much food for me."

"Don't worry," Ty said over his shoulder as he wove his way back to the food-laden table. "I'll eat whatever you can't finish."

That. That right there. That was why I loved him. He was always putting other people first. I didn't know a better person anywhere and, because of that, couldn't imagine ever loving someone who wasn't him.

CHAPTER

Thirty-Five

After we'd all eaten copious amounts of food and the Tyler family had bid us farewell for the afternoon, Dad donned a Santa hat and deposited green elf hats on top of Arlo and Paton. Then he sat himself down in the rocking chair next to our Christmas tree and chose presents for Arlo and Paton to hand deliver around the room. With all of us calling and pointing the way, Arlo could mostly be relied upon to get his present to the right person. Without fail though, Paton would toddle any present she picked up over to her mummy. Every single time. It was so freaking adorable.

Veronica and Mark's gift to me eventually made its way around the living room and into my hands. It was a pair of wireless earbuds for running. I didn't usually listen to music when I ran, but with the new earbuds I'd be willing to give it a try. Maybe I'd try to find music to match my mood each morning so that I could embrace my feelings while I ran instead of outpacing them.

I was watching Melody open her present from Gretchen when Arlo charged up to me holding the silver box Ty had brought over earlier. I had figured it was a gift box of biscuits or something from his family to ours, so my heart did a little thrill when I read the label:

Merry Christmas Nova
♡ From Ty

With extreme care, I peeled all of the tape off the paper and then unwrapped the gift. Inside, I found a nondescript black box with a flap at one end. I jimmied it open and peered inside. It held some kind of book. Wedging my fingers inside, I pulled the book out, which turned out to be a sparkly gold photo album. Its title read, **The Life, Love, and Friendships of Nova Brie Samson**, and was typed above a grinning photo of me and Skye.

"Oh…" I gasped, bringing my hand up to my mouth in a poor attempt to contain my emotion. "Oh... wow."

With shaking fingers, I turned to the first page of the album. It was printed with baby photos of me, Ty, and Alex being looked after by Veronica.

I kept turning the pages, almost in slow motion, as more precious memories were revealed. The album appeared to be in chronological order, with my birthday parties marking the division between one year and the next. Photos of me, Ty, Alex, and my sisters dominated the earlier birthdays, but Skye joined the photo progression from my ninth birthday onwards, and then Peter and Matthias began showing up when I reached high school age.

As well as birthday shots, the album had captured various events over the years, like *Weetbix* Triathlons, surfing lessons, rugby games, picnics at the beach, bush walks, camping holidays, and more. Towards the back of the book, I found a page formatted like a newspaper and dedicated to the most recent Secondary Schools Athletics Championships. There were several photos of me crossing finish lines. One was captioned: **Nova takes no prisoners on the 1200 metres;** Another: **Nova makes winning the 900 metres look easy;** And the final shot read: **Victory is guaranteed for long-distance running champion, Nova**

Samson, on the 1500 metres.

The athletics page even included a smiling selfie of Ty with his arms around both of my parents. He must have taken it when I went to use the bathroom in my effort to avoid him. All this he'd done for me when I wasn't even speaking to him. Why?

I turned to the last page of the album and found several photos of Peter, Matthias, and me that Ty had taken at Kitekite Falls. The last page also included a photo of my entire family, a photo of Ty's entire family, and a photo of Pastor Bailor and his wife, Louise. A message box in the middle of all the photos read: **Skye may be gone, but you, Nova Brie Samson, are still here and will never be alone. We love you to the stars and back.**

I was crying when I closed the album and looked up to find my entire family watching me.

"What have you got there, Nova Brie?" Dad asked, leaning forward on his rocking chair with interest.

"It's a photo album from Ty," I cried. "And it's absolutely amazing. Would you mind if I popped over to his house to thank him for it?"

"Not at all, sweetheart." Dad smiled, and then looked over at Mum and waggled his eyebrows.

I didn't have time to deal with that. My need to thank Ty was almost desperate. I ran out of the house and across the road barefoot, clutching the gold photo album to my heart. My knock on the Tylers' front door was as erratic as my heartbeat. I'm not even sure why I knocked. I guess the moment felt too important for me to just barge in.

James Tyler opened the front door, and his gaze immediately dropped to the photo album in my hands. "Ah, I see you got the gift." He nodded, a smile playing over his lips. "Come in, Nova. Andrew's out back."

I left Mr Tyler and sprinted down the hall, past Ty's bedroom and through the family room at the end of the house. The ranch slider opened to the Tylers' deck and tree-enclosed backyard, but I halted before stepping outside. Ty was lounging on a hammock hooked between two sprawling titoki trees. His guitar rested on his chest, and he strummed it idly. He wore the same fitted shirt and trousers as earlier, but he'd loosened the top few buttons of his shirt, and a cool breeze was playing across his chest.

I watched him for a few more moments, appreciating the sight of him. He looked so relaxed and happy. I almost didn't want to interrupt, but this was important. I really needed to thank him. With a difficult swallow, I stepped forward onto his sunlit deck.

Ty immediately registered my presence and launched himself to sitting, almost tipping out of the hammock as he did so. It was such a marked change from his relaxed posture of moments ago, that I laughed through the tears that were once again pouring down my face.

"This," I held up the photo album in front of me, "is the most precious gift anyone has ever given me. I don't even know how to thank you for it, but thank you."

"You don't need to thank me." Ty shook his head and held up a hand. He rose smoothly to his feet and placed the guitar behind him on the hammock.

"But this must've taken you hours." I stared down at the large album, which was at least 60 pages long.

"A couple of months, actually." He shrugged. "But that's neither here nor there."

I took a step towards him, the album still clutched in my grip. "What even made you think to do this?"

Ty leaned his shoulder against the trunk of one of the titoki trees and said, "After Skye died, I started putting together a photo album of her to give to her parents. A pathetic attempt at making amends." He shrugged self-mockingly. "But there were so many photos of you mixed in with the photos of Skye, and, since you'd completely disappeared on me, I started making an album for you too. It was my idiotic way of holding onto hope. I kept thinking that someone with so many happy memories and so much love surrounding her would surely return to us eventually. The fact you came back at all felt like a complete miracle."

I was overcome. Nothing was as precious as this – the realisation that he was absolutely my truest friend. No one had ever cared about me the way he did. I didn't deserve him. Not even close. But at least I could thank him for this gift.

"Thank you," I struggled to speak, my chest heaving like I'd just run the entire ridgeline of the Waitakere Ranges. "The fact you made this for me when I was behaving so horribly towards you is just... I don't even know how to describe it. Andrew Tyler, you are the best person I know. Thank you for putting up with me, even when I don't deserve it. Thank you for being my truest friend."

Before I could second-guess myself, I dropped the photo album onto the hammock beside his guitar and wrapped my arms around Ty in the best hug of my life – one filled with pure love.

CHAPTER
Thirty-Six

Falling deeper and deeper into love was like a slow descent into madness. My body no longer reacted to usual things in its usual way. A casual smile from Ty turned my fingers buttery, my skin hot, my voice breathless, and my thoughts jumbled. Once faithful to my command, my body had switched allegiance to the one it yearned for more than anything else.

Andrew Tyler, who had offered me the gift of his unwavering friendship – had in fact only ever offered me his friendship – was killing me with his kindness just as surely as he was bringing me alive with it.

I survived the rest of the summer through sheer gritted-teeth force of will. It seemed like most of my days intersected with Ty's at some point or another, and I grieved the relationship I wanted with him all while celebrating the one I did have.

Fortunately, my Year 12 accounting results came back and they were excellent, which meant Dad gave me the promised part-time job at his engineering firm. I worked three days a week for the rest of January, helping to cover for staff who were away on holiday. Dad said that when school started back, I would still be able to do some work from home in the evenings. It was the perfect arrangement.

In the meantime, I was seeing Ty in all the downtime I did have, and it was getting harder and harder to contain my feelings for him.

To help me process everything, I ran bubble baths more often than I probably should have, what with the Auckland water shortage going on that summer. It was totally worth it though, since it was during one of those baths that I realised something important. I was remembering what it had been like learning to surf with Ty – how he had always cheered me on exuberantly whenever I caught a wave, and how he had always rushed over to check whether I was okay if I got dumped by one. Looking back, I realised he had probably slowed down his own surfing progress with how attentive he'd been to me, but it had made all the difference for me out there. He had given me the confidence to learn that hair-raising sport, and I had loved him for it. I had always loved him.

I had loved him, but never named it as love because Skye told me about her crush on Ty almost as soon as I met her, and I had been desperate to keep her in my life. I'd been so lonely when I met her. Veronica had moved down to Palmerston North the year before, and I'd spent the time since then barricading my heart, pretending I didn't miss Veronica and didn't care that I didn't have any female friends at school.

But then Skye singled me out for friendship on her first day, and I was so relieved, I did whatever I could to prove to her I was worth keeping around. In my efforts to please Skye, I had ignored anything that might clash with her wants. I'd become more in tune with Skye's wishes than my own. My feelings for Ty would certainly have caused problems with Skye, so I had pretended I didn't have any. I had pretended so hard, I'd actually convinced myself I didn't.

I must have been comfortable enough in my friendship with Skye by my 16th birthday that my feelings for Ty were able to emerge again, but still, I never would have thought to act on them when Skye's feelings for Ty seemed so much more valid than my own.

Just imagine if I had acted on them. Imagine if I had stayed on that dance floor instead of obediently sitting down when Skye told me to. Imagine if I had danced with Ty that night. Everything might have been different.

But for me to have done that, I would have had to expect Skye to set aside her feelings for Ty, and that was something I would never have asked her to do. Why did it seem so much more acceptable for me to set aside my wants and desires than for Skye to set aside hers? Why did I still think my feelings weren't as valid or as important as hers? Deep down inside, did I think Skye's life had more worth than mine? Did I still think I was unworthy of love?

Cocooned in my bubble bath that night, I prayed to God, asking him to help me see my worth through his eyes. Then I reminded myself of all the things the Bible taught me about myself: God loved me; I was made in his image; I had been adopted into his family; I had been clothed in the righteousness of Christ; I had been forgiven; I had been saved from the penalty of sin; I was being redeemed.

My life had just as much worth as every other person God had made. Now, I needed to start living like it did.

And that process was about to happen in front of a thousand of my peers at *Laingholm High School*, an incredibly awkward place for me to return to after the way I'd behaved at the end of last year.

After Skye's death, I'd drifted through school like a phantom – looking at no one, talking to no one, just getting through my classes as best I could.

Everyone had been shocked when Skye died. Nobody expected a vibrant girl like her to just… stop living. But then, degree-by-degree, they'd got used to it as other things had taken centre stage in their lives.

I would look around me at all the familiar-but-strange faces and think, *I really should try and make some new female friends.* But then I'd feel guilty, like, *where's my loyalty?* If Skye was still alive, I wouldn't be bothering with any of these girls. I had already gone through four years of high school without getting to know them. If I talked to them now, I'd just be a faking faker.

So, I kept spinning around in these mental circles, getting nowhere, talking to no one. And just like with Skye, people forgot I existed.

CHAPTER

Thirty-Seven

But I was still here. And I didn't want to be a ghost anymore.

CHAPTER
Thirty-Eight

"Hey, Meg," I greeted my dainty classmate, who was walking into the same economics room as me on our first full day of Year 13. "How were your holidays?"

"Ahh…" Meg Hammond's pearlescent eyes darted right towards her bushy-haired friend, Sadie Harvey, before she answered, "Hey, Nova. Ah, they were good. Real good. How were yours?"

I breathed a sigh of relief at the fact Meg knew my name at least, even if she seemed super awkward about talking to me. Taking the name thing as a good sign, I sat down in the same row of desks as her and Sadie. "Pretty good. I painted a house, of all things."

"Huh." Meg seemed surprised. "Like, for *Habitat for Humanity* or something?"

"No, just for a friend. It felt good to be doing something, y'know. Took my mind off things."

"Yeah, I can imagine," Meg said awkwardly, but not unkindly.

Sadie leaned around Meg to say, "We were so sorry about what happened to Skye. I know you two were super close. If there's anything we can do for you, please let us know."

"Thanks." I smiled, even though I had no idea what I was supposed to ask for.

Grappling for another conversation topic – one not so fraught with awkwardness – I asked, "So, are you ladies ready for Year 13?"

"Are we ever?" Sadie exclaimed, leaning forward on her desk again to talk to me. "We're going to slay it. Aren't we Meg? Bring it, baby."

I laughed at her enthusiasm. Most people acted like school was the lamest thing ever; I loved that she wasn't afraid to actually try and let people see her trying.

Our economics teacher, Whaea Ariana, called the class to attention then, so our conversation finished, but at least I'd had one.

And I kept on talking to people for the rest of the day – striking up conversations in all of my classes to a mixed reception of raised eyebrows and surprised smiles. None of the conversations really led anywhere, so I still felt totally on the outside of things, especially when kids started scrolling through their phones, exclaiming over photos of parties and holidays that hadn't included me.

I bumped into Ty in one of the breaks between classes, and he stopped to ask how my day was going. My heart jittered oddly at being in his presence again, but I remained cool and told him about my spectacularly failing social experiment.

"Rome wasn't built in a day," he replied sagely, flashing a mega-bright grin my way.

"Thanks, Wise Old Elf." I laughed, feeling about a thousand times better than I had all day, just for being in his company.

"And hey, you've always got me," he reminded me. "I know I'm not so good with all the makeup and false eyelash convos, but I'm still your friend. That's not nothing."

"Yeah. That's not nothing," I agreed. It was far more than he'd ever know.

Of all the people I chatted to in my first week back, Meg and

Sadie were my favourites, so in our economics class on Friday I finally dared to ask, "What are you girls doing for lunch today?"

"Oh! Em! Gee!" Sadie of the big hair replied way more enthusiastically than I'd been expecting. "I'm so glad you reminded me. I've been meaning to ask you all week whether you'd model for my photography project this term."

"Uh, why me?"

"Your look is like completely stellar for it. Believe me."

"Ohhhhkaay, that sounds fun," I agreed, lying through my teeth so we could keep making headway on the friends thing. "Where should I meet you?"

"In the bathroom next to the staffroom would be primo."

"Cool, I'll see you there."

Apparently, we were meeting in the only decent bathroom in the school so Meg could touch up my makeup for Sadie's photo shoot. I wasn't wearing any makeup to begin with, to which Meg just said, "You're the perfect blank canvas."

"Thanks, I think," I said as she pencilled in my eyebrows.

"You've got great proportions, so everything I'm doing today is just about playing up your natural features."

"Okay. That sounds alright," I said, trying not to twitch as she dabbed luminiser into the corner of my right eye.

In the bathroom mirror, I watched my appearance come into focus under her skilful touch. It was an amazing transformation. My oval face, which had begun to get gaunt after Skye's death, had filled out a little over the summer and now, with Meg's makeup, actually looked radiant. My cheekbones were smoothly defined in a way that made them jut out without looking too sharp. My eyes seemed to be twice their normal size (although somehow sultrier for it); and my lips were so pouty and soft, I kept touching them to check they were real.

"What is this sorcery?" I whistled when Meg finally proclaimed herself finished.

"*YouTube* has *the* best makeup tutorials." She smiled proudly. "I can show you my faves if you like."

"Okay, thanks." It was obvious I needed to do some serious upskilling on the makeup front. Plain mascara wasn't going to cut it around a girl like this.

"Meg, that took way longer than 10 minutes," Sadie started to complain, but then saw Meg's sour expression and quickly added, "I mean, Nova looks awesome, don't get me wrong – but we're going to have to book it if we want to get any decent shots before the bell goes."

"Hey, don't stress," I said. "If you don't get what you need today, I'd be happy to model for you again. My schedule's wide open. You just say the word, and I'll say, 'cheese.'"

"Ha! I like this girl." Sadie grinned.

Ten minutes later, I was seriously regretting the whole modelling thing.

Sadie, it turned out, was an OTT perfectionist when it came to photography. She took, The. Exact. Same. Photo. Literally fifty times. Not even exaggerating. And for every single one of those photos I was supposed to look simultaneously sad and expectant, but also a little whimsical and tortured. What did that even mean?

Ty walked past with the guys while I was sadly, expectantly, whimsically, torturedly leaning against a tree. Thankfully he didn't see me, but Sadie snapped off photo number 51 and said, "That's the one. We're done for today." She spun around to figure out what had caught my eye and, when she saw Ty, turned back to me with a curious look in her grey eyes.

I stared back at her, wide and unblinking. *Nothing to see here. Nothing at all.*

Clearly, my innocent act didn't fool her for one second because, at lunch on Monday, I came out from my bathroom makeover with Meg to discover that Sadie had roped Ty into modelling too!

This time Sadie got me to lean against the same tree as on Friday, but she took her photos from behind my shoulder, focusing on Ty as he walked past down the concrete pathway. Sadie directed him to look straight ahead for all of the photos except the last couple, in which she asked him to turn his head and look at me.

"Perfect!" Sadie exclaimed after the first take. "Thanks for your help, Ty. You're officially dismissed."

"You're very welcome." He bowed with a flourish and then winked at me before taking off to find Peter and Matthias.

"So, you and Andrew Tyler, huh?" Sadie whistled.

"What?" I spluttered as Meg looked between Sadie and me with half-suppressed glee.

"Don't even bother denying it; I have photographic proof." Sadie pressed a button on her camera and held it up so I could see the screen. Scrolling through the identical photos she'd taken of me on Friday she commented, "Nova looking bored. Nova looking uncomfortable. Nova looking constipated...." On through all 50 of them until she got to number 51 and said... "Nova looking devastated by love."

"Oh my gosh," I whispered, stunned, because she was totally right. My eyes were practically shouting my feelings for Ty in that last shot. Love. Longing. Guilt. It was all there for anyone to see. Had *he* seen it?

"And now I present you with Exhibit B." Sadie scrolled through today's series of photos of Ty. "Walking. Walking. Walking. Turning his head. Looking at my girl, Nova. Fiercely in love with my girl, Nova. More walking."

Meg, beside me, nodded her head, and I started to wonder... could it be true?

"You don't think he was just acting, you know, for the scene?" I asked Sadie.

"I didn't give him any directions other than to walk and look at you. That was all him, baby."

"Oh my gosh," I whispered again, slumping against the tree. This could change everything.

"Is this one of those post-death love things?" Sadie asked. "You know, where two people bond over the death of a loved one?"

"Sadie!" Meg slapped a hand over Sadie's mouth, then turned to me and said, "I'm so sorry about her. She has *no* filter."

"It's okay," I said. "I've been wanting to talk to someone about this, but the last person I told didn't exactly keep it a secret, like I asked him to."

"Ohhh!" Meg dropped her hand from Sadie's mouth and looked at me like she desperately wanted me to spill my secrets. "Soooo.... *is* it a post-death/celebration-of-life love thing?"

"Not on my part." I shrugged. "I knew I had feelings for Ty a long time before Skye died. I probably had them my whole life but just suppressed them out of loyalty to Skye."

"Wow, you're a good friend," Meg said, patting my arm.

"Not such a good friend." I shook my head. "I mean, I'm completely obsessing over my dead best friend's boyfriend. It's so messed up."

"But do you think you'll do something about it anyway?" Meg asked. "Or do you feel too guilty?"

"I've been trying to get brave enough to do something about it all summer, but I never really thought I had a chance with Ty until you showed me that photo just now. He's never made a move, so maybe *he* feels too guilty." I dared to hope. "What would you girls do if you were me?"

Sadie clicked her fingers. "I'd snap that up so fast, all the volcanoes in Auckland would spontaneously erupt."

"I wish I had your confidence." I played with a jagged thumbnail.

"Don't worry," Meg whispered, conspiratorially. "Sadie's all talk. She doesn't even have a boyfriend."

"Hey. I'm standing right here." Sadie flicked her frizzy brown hair over her shoulder. Her expression was so outraged, we all laughed until the bell had us rounding up our things and parting ways for our next classes.

I was in a daze for the rest of the day, barely registering anything my teachers said. If the girls were right – if Ty really did have feelings for me – then I needed to face my fears and actually talk to him about it.

CHAPTER

Thirty-Nine

It never really cooled down in February, even overnight, but at least early morning was slightly less hot, making running bearable. Now that school had started back up, Ty and I resumed our Saturday morning runs.

He never complained about the heat or the humidity, even when it coated him in a sticky second layer. He was there on my porch before dawn every morning, faithfully waiting for me to emerge from my house. The way his face lit up when I opened my front door was better than any sunrise. And now I wondered if there was more behind his smile than I had ever realised. It was time to woman-up and find out for sure.

The morning after the photographic revelations, Ty and I ran all the way to Laingholm Beach, where the sun lifted its head over the horizon in a friendly *good morning*. I was listening to power ballads through my ear pods as we ran, trying to build up the courage to talk to Ty.

By the time we got to the beach, neither of us was in any rush to tackle the hill back home, so we took our time stretching against one of the wooden picnic tables that overlooked the beach.

Ducks slept on the grass a few metres away, looking like

Beatrix Potter illustrations with their heads tucked prettily under their wings. Their storybook nature provided the illusion we were standing in our own magical world, and that gave me the courage to ask Ty something that had been gnawing at me since Skye's death, even if it wasn't *the* question I needed to ask him.

"I know this is pretty random," I said as I stretched a hamstring, "but Skye texted me just before she died, saying she wanted to talk to me. You were with her at the time. Do you remember what she wanted to talk to me about?"

Silence.

And then Ty's breath huffed into the warm morning air.

"Yeah, I think I do." He turned away to stretch his shoulders.

"Oh, that's great." I smiled and leaned sideways into a stretch while I waited for him to carry on. When Ty remained silent, I prodded him, "Sooo, what was it about?"

The silence stretched out for another half minute before he finally muttered, "We had a fight."

"When?"

"That night. On Lion Rock."

"What were you fighting about?"

He exhaled for so long, I almost didn't catch the word he slotted onto the end of it – "You."

"Meeee?" I screeched. "Why were you fighting about me?"

Ty looked sideways at me, just a fleeting glance before he turned back to stare at the shelly beach in front of us, no longer pretending to stretch. "Because I said something stupid about how you would've loved to be there, since we had this perfect view of the stars and your name's Nova. You know, like supernova?"

"Okaaay… that doesn't sound so bad."

"Yeah, but Skye got mad about it and said something like, 'You do know my name's Skye, right? We're literally looking at the sky and instead of thinking about me, you've made some random connection to Nova. Do you even realise how often you talk about her? Are you in love with her or something?'"

I almost laughed. "Why was she even thinking that? You guys were celebrating your one-year anniversary."

"Yeah, we were. Aaand… she was right. I'd spent the whole day wishing you were there with me instead of her."

"WHAT?" I shouted, startling the ducks awake. "Why?"

"Because…" He shrugged, then bit down on his bottom lip as he turned around to look at me with dark eyes. "Do you really want to know? There's no going back from this once you do."

I wanted to know. Of course, I wanted to know, but this wasn't how I'd thought the truth would unfold. It hadn't occurred to me that Ty's feelings for me could have pre-dated Skye's death – or that she might have known about them.

I squeezed my hands under my armpits to steady myself for whatever Ty was about to reveal and then said, "Yeah, I want to know." If my conversation with Melody had taught me anything, it was that I couldn't run from the truth.

Ty gazed down at me and several expressions warred across his face before he cleared his throat and said, "I've always had a thing for you."

Oh. My.

"Always?" My breath was a feather.

"Well, I guess officially since I was old enough to understand what the thing that I was feeling for you was," he breathed back.

"Wait." One of my hands floated up between us with a mind of its own. "That's a long time to like me and keep it a secret. How did I not know about this?"

"You tell me." He shrugged and slid into the bench across the table from me. "It was exactly like this. Years spent just like this. My heart dying inside of my chest because the girl I dreamed about only ever saw me as a brother. Never looked at me with anything close to… to what I felt for her. So, I tried to get over you." He tilted his head back to stare at the sky for a few seconds before meeting my gaze once more. "I wasn't planning on getting over you with Skye, though. That part was an accident, as you know. When we got back to the table the night of your 16th, and she told everyone we were going out, you were beaming like it was the best news ever. You weren't even the slightest bit jealous, and I knew then that I'd never had a chance with you, so I just… went along with it."

Oh man. What a mess I'd made of things at my 16th birthday. Everything could have been different, if only I had stood up for myself.

But now I wanted to know more about the night Skye had died. They had been fighting?

"So what happened at your anniversary? You said you'd been wishing it was me there that day with you?"

Ty propped his elbows up on the table and rubbed his eyes with both hands, looking utterly worn out. He didn't hold back from answering me though. He was braver than me in that respect. "A whole year, Nova. Skye and I were celebrating a whole year together. That's a seriously long time for kids our age. And it got me thinking about where we were heading, you know? Everyone was talking about us like we were this old married couple. I *felt* like an old married couple. But the thing was, every time I pictured my future, I saw your face in it. Not hers. I always have. So, what the hell was I doing with her?" He looked directly into my eyes then, perhaps hoping I'd answer his rhetorical question.

"Oh, Ty," I sighed, and I wasn't sure if I was sighing for him, for Skye, or for myself. "Skye chose you," I tried to explain. "The first day we met, she told me she was going to marry you one day. And I was so in awe of her, I just accepted it as fact. I never let myself see you as anyone's but Skye's."

"Never?" he asked, dropping his head, and his sadness pulled at my heart.

"Never… until the night of my 16th birthday," I added, and

Ty flicked his head back up, hope warming his toffee-brown eyes for the first time that morning. "I was just figuring out that I had feelings for you when you got together with Skye. I did my best to be happy for you both, but it wasn't an easy year for me. I hope I didn't do anything to make Skye suspicious though."

"No, trust me. Neither of us suspected you had any feelings for me," Ty said, looking a little dazed by hope now that he knew I actually did.

"Good," I said. "That's good. So then, if it's not too hard to talk about, could you please tell me what happened the night she died?"

"Okay." Ty straightened up and continued recounting the events of that night. "Well, after Skye accused me of being in love with you, I didn't deny it, which, in hindsight, might have been a mistake because she went flying down Lion Rock and disappeared. I packed up all our things and found her waiting for me back at the car. 'Take me home,' she ordered.

"We were driving home when she grabbed her phone out of my bag and texted you. I saw your name on the screen and asked her what she'd said to you. 'I told her we need to talk,' Skye said.

"I begged her, 'Please don't bring Nova into this,' and she replied, 'Even now, your first instinct is to protect Nova.'

"'I'm not protecting her,' I said, 'she just doesn't know anything about this and she doesn't need to. She doesn't have feelings for me.'

"'But you have feelings for her?' Skye demanded to know.

"'Maybe,' I said. 'Look, it doesn't matter. It's not in the cards for me and her.'

"'So, what? I'm your consolation prize?' Skye asked, and I realised how this must have felt for her. Your reply came through then and Skye started texting you back. I tried to grab the phone off her and was so focused on that, I didn't see the corner. That's when we crashed."

"Oh. My. Gosh," I gasped, surprised frost didn't pour out of my lungs, I was that chilled by his revelation. Skye had spent her last moments on earth fighting with Ty about me. And I'd had no idea. "Why didn't you tell me this months ago?"

"When would I have told you?" Ty asked bitterly. "When you were ignoring me, or when I was desperately trying to win you back? Neither time would have benefited from this particular revelation. Even now, I tell you after we've spent the whole summer together, and you're staring at me like you don't know who I am."

"Ty! You've got to understand what a shock this is for me. I need to process my part in all of this. Because even though neither of you knew it, I did have feelings for you – the whole time Skye was dating you. Directly or indirectly, I did play a role in her death. And since Skye's gone, there's no way I can work it out with her, or apologise."

"You're right." Ty pressed his lips together. "Skye is gone. But I'm standing right here, and you finally know how I feel about you, so can't we sort out this thing between us, once and for all?"

"I'm so sorry," I shook my head, "but I really need time to think."

And then I did the thing I did best. I ran.

CHAPTER
Forty

There are a lot of sucky things about death, but the suckiest one has to be all the unsorted garbage that just stews away, getting smellier by the day. All it takes is a gentle nudge when you least expect it, and the filth comes bursting out.

This situation with me, Ty, and Skye had been rotting away for far too long, and it was time I cleared the air with Skye. Unfortunately, she was dead, which made that rather difficult.

I ran away from Ty after our conversation that morning, too upset to slow down for him on the return journey from Laingholm Beach. I looked back over my shoulder once, but he didn't even try to follow me. He just stood there on the beach, watching me go with a desolate expression crushing his too-beautiful face. It only added to my state of guilt, and I ran even faster, falling back on my old instinct to flee from pain.

I had unwittingly played a part in Skye's death. My best friend was gone because she was fighting with her boyfriend over me. It was too much to bear.

I wanted to go to the last place Skye had really been alive – Piha – so I could attempt to talk to her somehow. I didn't have any clue how much people in heaven saw of life on earth, but I hoped an angel would open up a portal or something so Skye could hear me this one last time at least.

It took a good forty minutes to drive out to Piha in the car Mum and Dad had given me. When I got there, I slammed to a stop in the car park across the road from the beach and yanked out the picnic I'd prepared earlier.

As I crossed the black sand beach to get to Lion Rock, I passed another woman going for a stroll but didn't raise my hand in greeting like I normally would have. My insides were in too much turmoil. I was completely focused on the task in front of me.

I clambered fast up Lion Rock, not slowing down until I reached the same place where I'd found Ty sitting last year – the place I figured he'd taken Skye to on their anniversary date. Once there, I collapsed onto the grass in front of the stone bench, my picnic falling haphazardly onto the ground.

Taking a minute to look out at the roiling sea view in front of me and collect myself, I thought about what I wanted to say to Skye. Then, when I was ready, I carefully unpacked the *Marmite* and cheese sandwiches I'd prepared earlier and set them out on two plastic plates, one for me and one for Skye. Meeting with Skye like this, or at least attempting to, was a sacred moment in my life, and I wanted to signify that with a ritual of some sort. Preparing a meal for her felt like it might do that. A last supper of sorts.

I ate and imagined her eating, even as her sandwiches remained untouched. How many *Marmite* sandwiches had we eaten together in our lives? A few hundred at least.

"Skye," I said, after swallowing my last bite of sandwich and throwing hers onto the rocks in front of me. "I don't know how time works for you where you are, but down here you've been gone for four months. That probably seems like the blink of an eye to you now that you have all of eternity to enjoy but, believe me, it has felt endless. I've missed you, but I've started to learn to live without you, even though that feels so wrong.

"A lot has changed since you died. For one, I stopped denying that I have feelings for Ty. Well, I tried to deny it for a little while by staying away from him, but that didn't work out so well, for either of us. Apparently, he has feelings for me too.

"I'm sorry for falling for the guy you were in love with. I tried my best to be a loyal friend to you and not resent what you had with him. I don't know if I was always successful with that, but please at least give me credit for trying. I hate that the last thing you did on earth was fight with Ty about me.

"Here's the thing though: I tried to be happy for you when you were with him, and now I'm really hoping you'll try to be happy for me too. I want to be with Ty. To be honest, I can't imagine being with anyone else. We always talked about me finding *The One*. Well, he's it.

"And I guess now, out of respect for you and our many years of friendship, I want to ask for your blessing. I'll pursue a relationship with Ty either way, but I'd feel so much happier knowing I had your approval."

I had been gazing out to the endless sea as I spoke to Skye, and continued to do so now, looking for some kind of sign that she'd heard me. But nothing changed.

I waited in silence for a few more minutes and then said, "I guess this was always a long shot, attempting to communicate with you like this. If you can hear me up there, please be happy for me, Skye."

And then, just as I began to gather my picnic things back together to get ready to leave, a small brown and gold piwakawaka landed on the rock in front of the sandwich I'd discarded. It pecked at the sandwich for a few seconds before flitting up and whirling about in a spectacular aerobatic display, spreading its fan-shaped tail like it was performing just for me. Almost as suddenly as it had appeared, it disappeared. And I remembered that in Māori lore, piwakawaka are believed to herald life or death through the gate.

It could have been a coincidence, but I chose to take the appearance of that piwakawaka as a sign and a blessing from my best friend.

"Thank you, Skye," I whispered, smiling, even as a few tears rolled down my cheeks. "I love you too. I'll go and live my life now."

CHAPTER
Forty-One

Feeling as free as a tui soaring over the treetops, I texted Ty: *Come meet me in the Kitekite Falls carpark. We need to talk.*

The entrance to Kitekite Falls was only a few minutes up the road from Piha Beach. Technically, Ty had promised me one last visit there before the summer was over, so I hoped he'd agree. The risk in asking him to meet me there was that he'd either have to drive himself – on the very road he'd crashed and killed Skye on – or he'd have to ask someone else to bring him, ruining his chance of speaking to me privately. I hoped he thought the risk of driving himself was worth it, and that he wasn't too upset with me for running away from him to ignore my request.

His reply came through a few minutes later: *I'll be there.*

I took a relieved breath and coasted down Lion Rock in a much different state of mind than I'd ascended it. Ty wouldn't be able to get to the falls carpark for at least another 40 minutes, so I gave myself time to walk along Piha's shoreline to the left of Lion Rock, hypnotised by the powerful waves rolling and crashing every few seconds. I was grateful for the salty sea spray, which helped cool me down in the hot afternoon sun.

Padding back through the blistering sand to my car, I deposited my picnic bag onto the passenger seat and then swung into the driver's seat, starting the car with the simple press of a button. Immediately, I had to wind down all the windows and crank the AC because my black EV had turned into a sauna while I'd been gone.

My feeling of calm started to dissipate as I anticipated the conversation with Ty ahead of me. First up, I needed to seriously apologise to him for running away that morning. And then I had to somehow segue into confessing just how strong my feelings for him really were. Communication had never been my strong suit. Skye had usually taken care of that for the both of us, so I was going to have to step up my game from here on in. At least journaling was helping me to figure out what I really thought about things these days so that I had something *to* communicate.

I drove the narrow road to the Kitekite Falls car park and got there with time to spare, which was lucky because it was completely full. I had to drive around for several minutes, stalking people until I found someone hopping into their car and exiting the dusty car park. I took their newly vacated spot and then decided to make myself useful by finding a carpark for Ty too.

Wandering around on foot, I spied a family climbing into their *Toyota Hilux*. I waited for them to leave and then stood in the middle of their car park, saving it for Ty. If he was driving himself all this way, he'd probably be stressed enough without needing to hunt down a car park on top of that. This was the very least I could do to help him out.

It was a shame there was no shade where I stood though, as I hadn't thought to bring a hat. I was wearing a sleeveless acrylic running top and stretchy three-quarter running pants over sneakers, and I could feel the sun cooking my shoulders. Luckily, I had brought sunblock, so I pulled it out of my backpack and rubbed it into my face, arms, and shoulders.

That helped kill a small piece of time, but it was still another ten sweltering minutes before Ty nosed his car into the dusty gravel car park.

He *was driving.*

I waved my arms over my head to get his attention. When his gaze found mine, I gestured for him to park where I was standing. He nodded and eased his way towards me, driving as slowly as my grandma Betty used to before she passed away. Hey, at least he was behind the wheel again. I walked backwards, using overdramatic arm gestures and knee bends to direct him into the parking space, pretending like I was one of those people who guide airplanes at the airport. It was my attempt to lighten the mood between us, and it must have worked because I saw Ty laughing as he parked.

And then he hopped out of the car, and I was instantly petrified.

"Hey," I squawked, the importance of this moment pressing against me on all sides.

"Hey," Ty replied, ultra-casual as he reached back into his car to grab his backpack. "You ready to go walking?" He was so much better at playing it cool than I was. No wonder I'd never cottoned on to his feelings for me.

"Yeah," I exhaled, feeling an immediate release of pressure thanks to his relaxed greeting. We didn't have to talk *quite* yet.

Ty was wearing a crisp t-shirt, board shorts, and fancy running shoes. He looked really good. Intimidating, but good. He slung his backpack over his shoulders and made for the entrance to the walking track. I hurried across the car park to catch up and fell into step beside him.

And then, before I could chicken out again, I put a hand on his forearm and pulled him to a stop.

"There's something I need to say," I said.

He nodded, looking uneasy.

"I'm sorry for running off this morning. I'd promised myself I would never do that to you again, and then I did it anyway. You didn't deserve it, and I'm sorry. Will you forgive me?"

His mouth flattened as he turned and started cleaning his shoes at the spray station that was there to protect the kauri trees. "If you'd asked me this earlier in the day, I would've been tempted to say no. I almost ignored your text asking me to meet you here. I mean, how much rejection can one guy take and keep coming back for more? But I realised that would be a chump move, so I'm here. Which means, yes, I forgive you. And I always will. Just please don't run away again. I'm not as tough as I look – especially where you're concerned."

I bit my bottom lip as I cleaned my shoes at the station next to his. I hated that I had hurt him again, when he had already suffered so much. "Okay, I promise. And thank you for coming to meet me here and for not giving up on me. I'll try not to make it so hard for you next time."

"I'd appreciate that." Ty smiled ruefully as we began walking along the wooden boardwalk that wound its ways into the trees.

We strolled in silence for a couple of minutes, just enjoying being there among the beautiful trees. The peace and tranquillity gave me the courage I needed to speak again. "There's something else I want to say," I announced as our walk took us under a canopy of nikau palms to the right of the rushing stream that was fed by the waterfall ahead.

"Yeah?" Ty cocked his head to the side.

"Yeah." I nodded. "I had a good talk with Skye up on Lion Rock just now, and I've made my peace with everything."

Ty arched a black eyebrow. "You… had a talk… with Skye?"

"Well, it was admittedly a one-sided conversation, but it still helped," I said as we began heading upwards on the walking track. "I realised it wasn't fair that I've been feeling guilty about liking you, when I think it was you and I who were meant to be together all along."

"You think that?" Ty stopped walking and looked at me, his head pulled back in amazement. "You think we're meant to be together?"

"Of course!" I exclaimed. "Don't you?"

"Hell yes. But I've *always* thought that – and it seemed like I was the only one who got the memo."

"Well, I got the memo, or whatever." I smiled. "It's why I stayed away from you after Skye's funeral. I felt so guilty."

"You did?" Ty looked puzzled, and I guess he was thinking back to the way I'd avoided him like he was contagious.

"Yeah, when you were looking all hot up on the stage, singing that song," I grinned at him, "and I realised just how much I wanted to be with you. And then I realised I was thinking that at your girlfriend's funeral, and that she happened to be my best friend. It was all so messed up."

"Messed up or not," he shook his head, "I've been waiting forever for you to realise that your boy next door was The Boy Next Door."

I snickered at that, but then Ty grabbed my hand and guided me towards a wooden bench we'd just come across at the top of the slope. Technically, we now had a view of the waterfall through the trees, but neither of us was looking at that.

Ty glanced down at our hands linked together, biting his bottom lip as he said, "So...." And then he trailed off.

"So...?" I echoed him.

"So..." he repeated, looking up at me as I nodded for him to continue. "You think we're meant to be together? Does that mean you... *want* to be together? Like, officially?"

"Yes! Definitely. Yes." I smiled at him.

"Excellent." Ty grinned and then used my hand, which he was still holding, to pull me back to my feet. "Let's go see a waterfall then. I remember it being quite beautiful."

CHAPTER

Forty-Two

Ty held my hand for the rest of the hike to the waterfall, and it felt like nothing I had expected it to. Whenever I'd seen people holding hands in the past, it had looked kind of comforting.

This did not feel comforting.

It felt electric. With Ty's long fingers threaded through my own, I discovered nerve endings between my finger joints I never knew existed.

His touch was doing strange things to my heart too, and I was having a hard time focusing on the simple task of walking on the rocky track. Everything felt new and heightened, awash in colour. It was totally overwhelming.

"M'lady," Ty said, acting the perfect gentleman as he helped me down the large slippery rocks to the waterhole at the base of the falls.

"You've never helped me down these rocks before," I pointed out.

"You've never been my girl before," he retorted, looking way too happy about calling me his girl. "Do you want to swim down here or up top?"

I looked around the crowded waterhole and then gazed up at the spectacular tumbling falls. "Up top for sure. I've been dreaming of going back there with you since the last time we were here."

"You have?" Ty shook his head like he wasn't certain he was awake.

"Definitely." I nudged him with my elbow. "So, get a move on, boyfriend." I had been wanting to say that word for a long time too. *Boyfriend.*

"Yes, ma'am." He saluted with his spare hand, flashing me a cheeky grin.

Still holding hands, we clambered across the stream and up the rocks to the gravel walking track that would lead us to the top of the waterfall. But before long, we came to a set of steps that was too narrow for us to climb side-by-side. Ty stopped walking and looked comically back and forth between our linked hands and the narrow steps. "Right then," he said. Letting go of my hand, he swung his backpack onto his front and crouched down in front of me. "Hop on, babe."

"What?" I snort-laughed. "You are *not* carrying me. And also, I didn't realise we were going to be one of those couples that calls each other babe."

Ty stood back up, apparently so he could gaze down at me through his inky black lashes. "Fair warning: I plan on calling you *all* the things, Nova. Because you *are* everything to me."

"Fine," my breath whistled out of me as I felt my cheeks redden. "You can carry me."

"You don't have to sound so pleased about it." Ty crouched down again, presenting his back to me, and I loved this. I loved that we were still *us* with each other, even if our entire relationship had changed.

I stepped towards him and gripped his broad shoulders, leaping lightly onto his back. He grabbed hold of my thighs and launched himself easily to his feet, like I weighed no more than his backpack. And then he began to climb.

I rested my head on his shoulder and breathed in his fresh, clean scent, feeling like I'd finally come home.

When we reached a wider section of walking track, Ty eased me back down to my feet and twined his hand through mine once more. Looking at me seriously, he said, "Just so you know, I'm never letting you go."

"That's alright with me," I squeezed his hand, "because now that I've got you, I'm never letting you go either."

He had to piggyback me twice more before we reached the summit, but we managed to keep our promise to hold onto each other. Anyone who saw us this time would have been in no doubt we were a couple.

At the top, we found a flat nook carved into the hillside to stash our things in. Ty removed his t-shirt and footwear while I watched on, a little breathless. It didn't seem possible, but he had toned up even more over the summer thanks to all our running, painting, and surfing. My boyfriend was shredded.

I'd been so busy watching him, I hadn't even removed my own shoes yet.

"You coming?" Ty asked me, launching smoothly to his feet.

"Uh." I regained consciousness. "Yeah. Just give me a minute."

I hadn't actually brought any togs with me since, when I'd planned my trip out to Piha, it had been all about talking to Skye, not about swimming in a waterfall. I considered swimming in my bra and knickers, but decided to stay in my athletic wear. It would dry fast enough.

I removed my shoes and socks, lining them up beside Ty's larger ones on the small bit of flat clay surface we'd found. "I'm ready."

"You're swimming in your clothes?" Ty asked, his forehead creasing.

"Yeah, it will be nice. Refreshing."

"Okay then." He twined his fingers back through mine and

helped me down the steep steps that some kind soul had cut into the clay bank.

"Thank you, good sir," I said.

Together, we reached the rocky ledge overlooking the first waterhole, and Ty said, "On my count, we jump. One. Two. Three."

Hand-in-hand, we leapt into the water, but had to let go as we swam back to the surface, both gasping at how cold it was. There was a marked difference between the hot air of that late summer afternoon and the chill of the waterhole. I pulled myself through the clear water, following Ty to the shallow end so we could climb out and descend into the smaller pool below, just like the last time. Our spot was empty, although I could see more people clambering around on the waterfall ahead.

Resting my arms on the ledge, I absorbed the stunning view in front of me and realised how incandescently happy I was. Ty was my boyfriend! I was his girlfriend! This was really happening. And then I glanced at Ty and saw that he wasn't looking at the view, he was watching me.

"Do you know what I was thinking about the last time we were here?" Ty asked, staring down at my mouth.

"Not a clue," I replied, although I was pretty sure I knew where he was going with this, judging by the direction of his gaze.

"I was thinking that if I didn't get to kiss your lips once before I died, I might actually die a tortured man."

"Just once, eh?" I arched an eyebrow at him, teasingly. "Well, I guess we'd better make it a good one then."

"Oh, it'll definitely be good," Ty murmured, reaching up to gently cup the side of my head and hook his fingers into my dripping hairline. He held my gaze for a long moment, and I felt myself drift closer to him, wanting to breathe him in. A smile twitched in the corner of his mouth as he ducked his head and finally, *finally* brushed his full lips across mine. I didn't see anything after that. My eyelids fluttered shut of their own accord.

Our first kiss was soft and sweet and yearning – everything I had ever hoped it would be. I sighed his name, and Ty captured the sound with his mouth, brushing his lips against mine again and again. And again.

Then, almost reverently, Ty slid two long fingers down my cheek and followed their path with his lips. "How are you so beautiful?" he murmured into my ear as I tilted my head to the side to give his mouth better access. A delightful shiver darted up my spine as his breath tickled the sensitive skin of my neck. I rubbed my face against his rough stubble, and the contrast between that and his breath on my skin was almost unbearably good.

Wanting to feel Ty's lips on mine again, I slid my arms around his broad shoulders and pulled him towards me. He made a sharp sound as we collided and immediately met my lips with his own, wrapping his arms around me like he couldn't get close enough. Our kisses changed in intensity, becoming more urgent as we drank each other in. I could feel Ty's heart pounding against my chest, and my own heart matched it beat for beat. Ty's warm hands stroked up and down my spine as our kiss became the culmination of all the weeks, months, and years we had spent longing for each other. Everything had been building towards this moment. Our patience was finally paying off.

Gasping for breath, we pulled away from each other, and I realised I was trembling. The water was the only thing holding me up. I was so unsteady, I felt like I needed to lie down. I gripped Ty's strong forearms for balance instead.

His dark eyes were glazed as he studied me, shaking his head in wonder. Leaning forward to brush a kiss against my forehead, he wrapped his arms around me and murmured into my shoulder, "Well, I got my kiss at last, but I think I might die a tortured man anyway. You are the sweetest thing. How am I ever going to get enough of you?"

"Don't," I replied, pushing out of his embrace so I could cup his face and bring his perfect lips down to mine again in a quick kiss. "Let's just agree right now to never get enough of each other."

"Deal," Ty said, turning his face to kiss the palm of my hand. "Easiest deal I've ever made. I already know I'll never get enough of you."

"Me neither. Ty?"

"Yeah?"

"I love you," I whispered, feeling shy but wanting to let him know my true feelings.

"Yeah?" Ty's grin lit his face.

"So much." I couldn't help but smile back at his look of pure joy.

"Well, I'm pretty sure you already know I love you, but I'm not sure you know how much," he said, tucking a loose strand of hair behind my ear.

"I know." I nodded.

"You do?"

"Yeah." I nodded again. "You love me better than I love myself."

Epilogue

A lot can change in a year. But some things never change.

When I opened my front door to greet Ty on my 18th birthday, he wore a fitted shirt and dress pants just like he'd worn on every birthday that had come before it. He also carried a beautifully wrapped gift in his hands, which he passed to me as he leaned down to kiss me on my cheek. "Happy Birthday, Nova," he murmured into my ear.

And then, I guess because he was finally allowed to say the thing he'd wanted to say at my last birthday, he sucked that irresistible bottom lip of his into his mouth and said, "You look stunning."

"Thank you." I beamed at him.

This year, I had put conscious effort into how I looked for my birthday party. I'd borrowed a bright green dress from Melody, who had way too many dresses anyway. I'd also asked Meg to do my hair and makeup. She was currently sitting in the lounge with Sadie, Matthias, and Peter, who'd all already arrived. I really should go back to them, but I wanted to spend another moment alone with Ty while I could.

"Did I ever tell you how grateful I am to your mama for making you dress up for my birthdays and kiss me on my cheek every year?" I asked, tilting my face up to kiss *him* on his clean-shaven jaw.

"Did I ever tell you it wasn't my mama who made me?" Ty grinned.

"Seriously?" I gasped, surprised *that* hadn't occurred to me. "It was all your idea?"

"Of course." He smiled sheepishly. "When else was I going to be allowed to kiss you?"

"Oh, Ty. That is the sweetest thing I've ever heard." Which wasn't technically true, since Ty told me sweet things all the time. He was such a kind and considerate boyfriend.

Our relationship definitely wasn't perfect – I still had days when I struggled with feeling unworthy of love, which made me doubt Ty's love for me. Ty had his own issues to deal with, thanks to lingering trauma from the way Skye had died, but we spent a lot of time talking through it all, and we tried our best to keep our relationship healthy by processing our feelings when they came up.

I tilted my face up to kiss Ty on the lips once, and then again for good measure. Taking hold of his hand and feeling closer to him than ever, I led him around the corner to the living room I'd decorated with fairy lights for the occasion.

We found Matthias eating all the chips while Peter hit on Meg. He had been trying to win her over since she and Sadie first started hanging out with us at school. I was pretty sure he would wear her down eventually, although Meg swore otherwise.

The six of us had gathered together for my birthday, and there, positioned with pride of place in the centre of the coffee table, was a scented candle I had lit for Skye.

It had been exactly one year since she'd died, and I could have chosen to spend the day mourning her, but, ever since that day up on Lion Rock eight months before, I'd decided that no one could live my life but me... and my life would always be worth living.

Acknowledgements

First and foremost, I'd like to thank God for giving people the ability to create and enjoy good books. Reading is one of my favourite things ever, but writing brings its own special joy.

Secondly, I'd like to thank my husband, Paul, and my children, Lily, Sophie, and James, for cheering me on and supporting my love of writing by giving me the time I needed to work on this book. You're the best family I could ever hope for. I love you to the university and back.

Thirdly, I want to thank everyone who took the time to give feedback on early drafts of *Ever Since that Day*. Charlotte Reynolds, Anna Richdale, Jodie Franklin, Beth Marshall, Faith Morrison, Lily Abrahams, Charis Abrahams, Mandy Abrahams, and Brent Abrahams – I gave careful consideration to everything you pointed out, and was so grateful to have your insights. Thank you! And an extra special thanks to my writing friend, Angela Armstrong. You have been my cheerleader and adviser for every step of this journey. I couldn't have done it without you. Thank you for your advice, feedback, and encouragement.

Fourthly, thank you to Malcolm Hicks for answering all of my questions about long distance running when I first came up with the idea for this book. Your insight was invaluable, since I can't imagine anything worse than running voluntarily.

Fifthly, thank you to Laura Good and Caitlin Tindall for

designing the book cover and layout of my dreams, and for being as excited about this project as I am.

And finally, thank you to everyone who has read and shared this book. You've made my writing dreams come true.

Ngā mihi nui!

About the Author

Emma Abrahams grew up in Auckland, New Zealand,
arguably one of the most beautiful cities in the world.
She quickly fell in love with words and the places they
could transport her to. Handy, since New Zealand is so
far away from anywhere else.

Emma completed a Bachelor of Communication Studies
at Auckland University of Technology, before marrying
the love of her life and having three precious children
with him. For many years, Emma fitted writing in
around homeschooling her children. Now, Emma works
as a school librarian, where she gets to share her love of
books with a new generation, while also crafting her own
stories on the side.

Author photograph taken by Nadine Canestri